"Those smell delicious..."

Lizzie placed one of the hot cookies on a napkin and set it in front of Paul. His eyes lit up in a look of sheer delight.

The smile on his face broadened as he said, "Ah, Lizzie, you do know the way to a hardworking man's heart."

She gasped and took a step back, and out of a long-practiced instinct her hand flew up to cover the scar on her face.

She wasn't trying to work her way into anyone's heart, least of all Paul's. He was her childhood friend.

"Lizzie." His tone softened. "I didn't mean to make you feel uncomfortable with my words. Please don't shy away from me."

Slowly, she lowered her hand.

"You don't need to hide your face from me, ever. I need you to understand that, Lizzie."

She gave him a slight nod, fighting the urge to cover her scar again.

And all the while she felt his gaze on her...

An Amazon top ten bestselling historical romance author, **Tracey J. Lyons** was a 2017 National Excellence in Romance Fiction Award finalist. She sold her first book on 9/9/99! A true Upstate New Yorker, Tracey believes you should write what you know. Tracey considers herself a small-town gal who writes small-town romances. She is making her contemporary romance debut with Harlequin's Love Inspired line. Visit www.traceyjlyons.com to learn more about her.

Books by Tracey J. Lyons

Love Inspired

A Love for Lizzie

A Love for Lizzie

Tracey J. Lyons

LOVE INSPIRED BOOKS

ISBN-13: 978-1-335-47926-6

A Love for Lizzie

This edition published by arrangement with Love Inspired Books.

www.Harlequin.com

Printed in U.S.A.

And be ye kind one to another, tenderhearted,
forgiving one another, even as God
for Christ's sake hath forgiven you.
—*Ephesians* 4:32

From the time I put the first word on the page
for this book, I knew without a doubt who it
would be dedicated to. This book is dedicated
to my friend and fellow author Amy Lamont,
who has shown more strength and courage
than anyone I know. You have inspired
so many of us with your journey.
Many, many blessings to you, my friend.

Acknowledgments

There are always so many people who are
part of the team it takes to make the
germ of an idea become a full-blown story.
First and foremost, I'd like to thank my agent,
Michelle Grajkowski, who puts up with all my
angst, and to all of my fellow Love Inspired
authors, you have opened up a whole new world
of support and friendship beyond what I could
have ever imagined. Thank you all so much.
To my editor, Melissa Endlich, thank you for
making my dream of becoming a Harlequin
author come true. To the fabulous team that
Harlequin has put together to get our work
out there in the world, you all deserve
a hearty round of applause.
And finally, to my husband, TJ,
I couldn't do any of this without you by my side.

Chapter One

Miller's Crossing, Chautauqua County, New York

"Good morning, Lizzie."

Her long-time neighbor and friend, Paul Burkholder, greeted Elizabeth Miller, or "Lizzie" as everyone called her, from the other side of the screen door on the front porch. A tall man with mahogany-brown hair and dark brown eyes, his head barely cleared the top of the door. He was holding his flat-brimmed straw hat in one hand and a bag in the other. He wore a blue work shirt and black pants with thin leather suspenders, the ends buttoned inside the waist of his pants, the typical everyday clothing of a Miller's Crossing Amish man.

His face was clean-shaven, void of the full beard that marked the married men. She'd always thought him to be handsome. At twenty-three he remained single, while most of his friends were getting married, though she'd heard rumors at the last frolic that he wanted to change all of that. Paul might look like many of the other men in their church district, but Lizzie knew this man had a big heart. Maybe sometimes too big of a heart. He'd stuck by her through thick and thin.

Even all the times she'd pushed him away.

Lizzie knew over the past week she'd been pushing at him extra hard. This time of year was always a difficult one for her and her family. Her gaze slid to the hook on the wall next to the door. The place where her *bruder*'s black hat still hung. She swung her attention back to the man standing on the porch. Concentrating on the present kept Lizzie from thinking about that long-ago day. A day she tried hard to forget. Yes, some of her memories of that day remained foggy, stuck somewhere deep in her mind, like a splinter that she couldn't get out. Still, the end result could never be changed; no matter what she remembered, her brother, David, would still be gone and she would have this mark seared on her face.

Paul rolled his shoulders, the strong muscles flexing beneath the cotton fabric of his light blue shirt. Lizzie's hand moved to cover the scar on her face. Beneath her fingertips she felt the raised flesh. The jagged cut ran three inches long, from the edge of her eyebrow to just below her cheekbone. Vanity held no place in her life or in her community, but still some days it was hard to accept reality. She had a disfigurement that couldn't be overlooked. Over the years the members of her community had done just that, continuing to love her and accept her through the flaws.

The *Englischers*, though, they were different. Some of them would openly stare at her when they stopped by her roadside stand to buy their fresh eggs. They were one of the reasons Lizzie didn't stray from the farm very often. She couldn't bear it when people stared at her. Their looks left her feeling ugly and unworthy.

She felt Paul's gaze on her.

"Lizzie?"

She heard his concern and looked up at him, keeping her face turned ever so slightly.

"You seemed to have gone off there for a minute."

"Do you know what today is?" The second she blurted out the question, she was filled with regrets. It didn't do a person good to dwell on the past, to dwell on things that couldn't be changed, to question the path that God had set forth for them.

Paul looked through the screen door at her, his eyes darkening with emotion. His nod was barely perceptible when he replied. "I do. Ten years to the day of the accident that took your *bruder*'s life and left you injured." His voice softened as he continued, "Lizzie, like you, I miss David every day. And like you, I wish we could have changed the outcome."

She held up her hand. There was no need for him to continue. She knew he was referring to his part in the day. He'd come to the barn just as she'd tried to get David to stop jumping off the hay bales. But David, who had always been the daring sibling, had insisted he could make it from the top all the way down to the bottom in one jump. She had tried her best to grab hold of his arm, but he'd already begun moving through the air when she'd caught hold of him.

Her body had been carried along with his as they'd tumbled down the bales. That was the last thing she remembered before waking up in the hospital. Lizzie pushed the dark memory away as best she could. She looked at Paul. Moving off to the side of the door, Lizzie turned her head ever so slightly to the right, hiding the scar. From the safety of the shadows, she looked up at him, watching as a soft summer breeze ruffled through his dark hair.

Though the Amish did not commemorate the anniversaries of one's death like some of the *Englischers* did, she herself always paused for a moment on this day to remember David. He would have been close to twenty-three years old. Three years older than she was right now.

Pushing aside the sadness in her heart, she said, "I'm sorry. I should have begun our conversation with '*Gut* morning, Paul. What brings you around this fine day?'"

Holding the brown paper bag up, he replied in his deep, rich voice, "I have something for you."

"You know I can't accept a gift from you."

"You don't even know what is inside of here," he said, swinging the bag back and forth in front of her.

She had to admit he had piqued her curiosity. "Tell me what you brought."

"I brought you some brushes and watercolor paints."

Lizzie didn't like the idea that Paul had gone out

of his way to spend his hard-earned money on something just for her. And considering that it wasn't useful to anyone else, she knew the paints and brushes would have to be kept out of sight.

Thinking how much trouble Paul's generosity could cause, Lizzie shook her head, saying, "*Nee.* You'll have to take these back to where you purchased them. I'm sure you can get your money back." Furrowing her brow, she gave him a stern look.

"I'll do no such thing. Besides, I found them at a yard sale, so there's no use in trying to return them. They only cost me a few dollars, Lizzie. And half of the paints have been used," he said. Then with a spark in his eyes, he added, "Think of this as my bringing you supplies for your art."

Lizzie had taken up artwork years ago. Sketching the surrounding landscapes had given her a bit of peace and helped to fill the void left behind after her brother's death. Since her *vader* would most certainly frown on using her time to dabble in something most Amish would consider frivolous, Lizzie managed to scrape together a few free hours each month to work on her craft. In her mind her drawings were no different from the beautiful quilts her friends made. Most sold them as a way to supplement their family's income. All of her drawings were carefully stored in a closet in her bedroom. As it was, Paul wouldn't even have known about her artwork except that he'd come upon her working on a new sketch at the edge of the back field last week.

The image she'd been drawing was of the freshly

mowed hayfield. She'd been drawing the soft, round bales of hay, trying to capture the feel of the image before her, of the golden hues against the dark earth and the sky being bathed in the soft colors of dusk. The black-and-white sketch hadn't done the scene justice, but Lizzie didn't have any colors to use on the picture. She'd captured the image as best she could, with her pencil on the heavy white paper.

Resting her head against the doorjamb, she let her imagination wander. The idea that she could add color to her sketches and breathe life into them had her pushing the door open a crack. Seeing the opportunity, Paul shoved the bag into her hand.

"I know you can make good use of these. Your drawings are amazing, Lizzie."

She felt the skin on her cheeks warm with a blush. Lizzie didn't get many compliments. *"Danke,"* she said, gripping the paper bag in her hand. "How is your family?"

Paul shrugged, answering, "They are fine. We've been busy at the shop."

Paul's family owned a cabinetmaking business. Even with him and his three *bruders* all working at the shop, they always seemed to be busy. All the more reason Lizzie appreciated the time he took to stop by to check on her family. There was only Lizzie left here to help on the farm. Her older sister, Mary, had married and moved away to her husband's church district last year. There were no other siblings left. Her *mudder* had been unable to have more children. Her *vader* worked from long before sunup to sundown, running their small dairy farm. Lizzie helped where she could, selling eggs, jams and baked goods at the roadside stand.

The farm life wasn't an easy one. Even so, she knew her *vader* wouldn't live his life any other way. She wished things were different. If she had a husband, he could help out. But Lizzie couldn't even imagine entering into a courtship. Absently she rubbed the side of her face. The scar was a constant reminder of the life she couldn't have. Most days she didn't even leave the farm. She felt safe and secure here, away from the prying eyes of those who wanted to see her face, those whose expressions carried all the questions of wanting to know what had happened to leave that mark on her.

Yet, Lizzie thought, she could be perfectly content to live out the rest of her life here, in quiet and safe solitude.

"What are your plans for today?" Paul asked.

Lizzie blinked, looking up at him, realizing the screen door still separated them. She didn't want him to think she was being rude, so she asked, "Would you like to come in for some coffee and a muffin? I baked blueberry ones earlier this morning."

"*Nee*. *Danke* for the offer, though. I need to get back to work. I just wanted to give you the paints in case you were planning on drawing today." Paul set his straw hat back on his head.

"*Danke* again for your thoughtfulness," Lizzie said, looking past him.

Her gaze settled on the big red barn, where she

knew her *vader* was finishing up with the morning milking. Her *mudder* had gone into the village of Clymer, a few miles from the house, to pick up some items from the Decker General Store. Cocking her head to one side, Lizzie looked through the dappled sunlight, beyond the shade of the big oak tree next to the house, and squinted her eyes, uncertain of what she was looking at.

"Paul, turn around and look down to the barn. Is that a cow I'm looking at?" she asked, pointing to a spot at the farleft corner of the barn, where the animal appeared to be munching on some grass outside of the fenced-off field.

Turning to look over his shoulder, Paul seemed to ponder her question and then said, "Lizzie, is your *vader* down at the barn?"

"*Ja*, he is supposed to be. Why do you ask?"

"Because there appears to be about half a dozen cows on this side of the fence."

"That is strange." She opened the door, stepping out to join Paul on the porch. "I think we should go see what's going on."

Tucking the bag into her apron pocket, she hurried along with him down the graveled pathway, across the driveway and to the barn, where they both stopped in front of the open door. Lizzie could see at least a dozen cows wandering about the yard surrounding the building. She turned to look up at Paul, whose gaze followed in the same direction as hers.

"Something's wrong. "There's no way your *vader* would let the cows roam free."

A shiver raced along her spine as she stepped behind him, following him into the dark coolness of the same building where her brother had plunged to his death ten years ago today. Sucking in a deep breath, Lizzie tried to swallow the panic welling up inside her.

"*Vader!* Are you in here?" Lizzie called out.

They stopped in the center of the large expanse. Sunlight streamed in through the slats of wood on the outside walls. Off to one side were the feed bins. There was no sign of her *vader* here.

"I think we should check the milking parlor," Lizzie said, putting her hand on Paul's arm, guiding him forward.

Thick dust motes stirred through the air as they made their way to the back of the building, where the milking parlor was located. Lizzie rubbed the end of her nose. The hay dust always made her want to sneeze. She held her breath, waiting for the sensation to pass. When it did, she took in a soft breath. Paul held the door to the parlor open, then nodded, indicating she could enter first.

"Ach! Nee!" Lizzie covered her hands over her face, not wanting to believe that what she was seeing in front of her could be real. Quickly she dropped her hands to her side and ran to where her *vader* lay on the cement floor, silent and still.

Paul pushed his way into the room, not that far behind Lizzie. His heart thudded in his chest when he saw Joseph Miller lying on his back on the floor.

Even from the distance of a few feet away, Paul could see the ashen color of the man's skin. He took in a breath and then gently but quickly moved Lizzie to one side so he could check on her *vader*'s condition. Kneeling beside Joseph, Paul placed his fingers alongside the man's neck, feeling the area where the carotid artery lay.

"Is he…?" Lizzie's voice was barely a whisper.

Paul held up his free hand, silencing her. He needed to concentrate. He moved his fingers up and down the side of the man's neck. At first he felt nothing, but then he felt a very faint throb. It wasn't much, but it was better than nothing.

"Lizzie, I need you to run up to the phone shack and call 911. Tell them you think your *vader* has suffered a heart attack." Even as Paul said the words, he couldn't be sure that was what had happened, but it would get the ambulance to arrive faster. "Tell them he is breathing, but it's very shallow."

He glanced up to find her still standing in the milking parlor, as if frozen in time. Tears rolled down her face, and her hands were knotted together in front of her apron. He could see her trembling. If her *vader* were to survive, Paul needed her help.

"Lizzie!" Hoping to jolt her into action, he shouted her name. "Lizzie! You need to go. Now!" Immediately Lizzie ran out the barn door.

The next few minutes were a blur. Joseph Miller lay on the hard floor of the barn, still as the air before a summer storm. Paul grew even more worried. He jostled the man's shoulder, calling out his name.

"Joseph! Can you hear me? Joseph!"

The man's eyelids fluttered and then stilled. Paul stayed beside the man, praying for his healing. The ambulance arrived, and after the paramedic did a quick assessment, he determined that Joseph needed to be transported immediately to the hospital in Jamestown, thirty miles away. Lizzie's mother, who'd been out running errands, came barreling toward the barn.

Pushing through the small circle of emergency responders, she cried out, "Paul! What's happening?"

He looked into eyes the same light blue color as Lizzie's. He saw Susan Miller's fear for her husband's health. Quietly he answered, "Mrs. Miller, I can't be sure. But the paramedic thinks it could be a heart attack."

The woman let out a sob and rushed alongside the gurney. Her midcalf-length black skirt flapped against her legs. "Joseph! Joseph!" she called out to her husband.

A younger medic caught up with her. "I can let you ride with your husband, but I need you to sit in the front. Do you think you can do that?" he asked.

Susan nodded, casting a glance around the tall man until her gaze found Lizzie. "Lizzie! I need you to come."

"I'm afraid we can only take one family member."

Lizzie's *mamm* looked as if she were about to burst into tears. Paul watched as she tucked her lower lip between her teeth, squared her shoulders and nodded at the man. Her hands trembled as she reached for the door.

Paul helped her into the front seat of the ambulance, making sure she had the seat belt firmly in place. "I'll see that she gets to the hospital."

"Run down to Helen Meyer's *haus*. Maybe she can help you get Lizzie to the hospital," Lizzie's *mamm* said.

"We need to get going," the driver said, putting the rig in gear.

Paul shut the door. Lizzie's mother smiled nervously from behind the window and nodded as they drove away.

Paul knew what had to be done. He would get Lizzie to the hospital. How could he not?

After the ambulance left, Paul realized he couldn't take the wagon into Jamestown. The trip would take a few hours by horse, and he couldn't be sure Lizzie's *vader* would survive. They needed to get there as quickly as possible. As Mrs. Miller suggested, he ended up running down to find their *Englisch* neighbor Helen Meyers, who was standing at the end of her driveway.

"I just saw the ambulance leave the Millers'. What's going on?"

"It looks like Joseph might have had a heart attack," Paul responded. Before he could even ask, she graciously offered to take them to the hospital.

"It was a blessing that I filled up my gas tank this morning."

Paul nodded politely. "I'll repay you for the gas."

"There's no need for that." She hastened to give him a smile. "We're neighbors and, *Englischer* or Plain, neighbors help each other out. Let's hurry—we don't want to keep Lizzie waiting."

He followed her to the back of the driveway and got into the passenger seat of the blue four-door sedan. They found Lizzie standing along the edge of the road, near the Millers' mailbox. Paul got out and opened the back door, letting Lizzie slide across the seat first. He joined her, barely closing the door before Mrs. Meyers sped off.

Paul turned his head to look at Lizzie. He could see the tight lines around her mouth. She kept her eyes focused straight ahead.

He started to reach out his hand to cover hers but thought better of it. Even though years had passed since the tragedy that shook the Miller family, there were days when Lizzie still seemed so fragile to him. Today would have been a rough day even without her *vader*'s heart attack.

"Today is the day my *bruder* died, and my *vader* suffers from a heart attack. I don't understand the workings of God."

"It's not for us to question his motives, Lizzie."

"I know." She turned to look out the window.

They rode the rest of the way in silence. Before they knew it, Helen pulled her car in front of the hospital entrance.

"I'll let you off here so you can hurry to the emergency room. I'm going to park in the main lot."

"Please, Mrs. Meyers, you don't need to stay. I will find a way home," Lizzie said.

"She's right, there's no need for you to spend your day here. I'll make sure Lizzie gets home. We appreciate your help." He thanked her again as they left the car.

He cupped Lizzie's elbow and escorted her through the automatic sliding doors. They whooshed closed behind them. He felt her tense up as people stared at them as they walked over to the reception area. His heart squeezed as he watched Lizzie tip her head down and raise her hand to cover her scarred face. The strongest urge to protect her welled up inside of him. He took a deep breath before coming to a stop at the receptionist's counter, which was closed off with big sliding glass windows.

Paul tapped lightly on the window, getting the young woman's attention. She gave him a hard look. Paul attempted a smile. She slid one of the panels open.

"May I help you?"

"My friend, Miss Miller's father, was brought in by ambulance a short time ago. We were hoping you could direct us to where we can find him."

"Can I have the name of the patient, please?"

"Joseph Miller."

The woman typed his name into the computer sitting on her desk, then slid a clipboard across the narrow counter space that separated them, saying, "I'll need you to sign in here, please. And then have a seat in the waiting area. I'll call you when you can go down to the Emergency Room."

"How long do you think it will be?" Lizzie asked.

"I'm not sure."

Paul picked up the clipboard and handed it to Lizzie, along with a pen. He waited for Lizzie to add her name and then did the same. When they were finished, she exchanged the list for two visitor stickers, which they both stuck to the front of their shirts. He turned and spotted two dark green vinyl chairs set apart from the main waiting area.

"Come on—" he nodded in that direction "—let's go over there to wait."

Lizzie went ahead of him and sank down into the first chair. He sat in the chair next to her. A long row of windows ran behind their backs. A low coffee table filled with dog-eared magazines separated them. His gaze settled on her. She sat on the edge of the cushioned seat, with her back hunched over and her hands clenched together on her lap. He felt so helpless and wanted to calm her nerves as best he could. He saw her take in a breath and then slowly exhale.

"Lizzie." He spoke her name in a low voice. "I'm sure your *vader* is in good hands. All will be well, I'm sure."

She pressed her lips together and nodded, keeping her eyes on the double doors at the far end of the room.

"I pray that he is. *Danke* for staying with me. I know you have other things you need to be doing," she said, keeping her voice low, as well.

Paul thought about how he'd originally planned to spend the day. For months now he'd had his mind set on breaking away from his family's furniture business. And he'd decided that this morning, after he'd gone to see Lizzie, would be the time he'd tell his *vader* about his plan to set up his own furniture shop. His *vader*'s furniture was very basic and serviceable. But Paul had always favored adding more detail to the pieces, while his *vader* liked to keep it plain and simple, a reflection of their way of life.

He'd been lucky to find a vacant storefront right next to the general store in the village of Clymer, a few miles south of their settlement. The rent on the space was good, too good to pass up. Not wanting to miss out, Paul had made a verbal agreement with the owner to lease the space. If everything went according to plan, he'd have the doors open as soon as possible. First he had to convince his *vader* to let him move forward. But deep down Paul knew he would risk the man's censure to follow his dream of owning his own business.

"I've heard rumors about you. About your plans for the future."

The sound of Lizzie's soft voice snapped him out of his reverie. "Who told you?"

"Though our land is vast, we live in a very close-knit community. Word gets out," Lizzie answered. She turned a thoughtful blue-eyed gaze to him. "Are you sure you want to break from your family business?"

He nodded. "I don't see it as breaking away. Maybe

the move could be more of an expansion of the business. I've started to pick out the pieces I'm going to sell at the new store. It's been a dream of mine for a very long time. Sort of like you and your paintings." He grinned at her.

"I don't do my paintings for profit."

"No, you don't. But I—" His explanation was interrupted when he heard Lizzie's name being called.

"Come on, I think there's some news." Paul guided her over to the reception area. Once there, the woman instructed them on how to get to the emergency room.

He started through the doors and turned back when he realized Lizzie wasn't with him. She stood in the doorway to the long corridor, pale as a ghost. Her blue eyes were wide as she stared down the hallway.

Rushing over to her, he took her trembling hands in his. "Lizzie, your *vader* is going to be all right. I know it. Joseph is a strong man. As strong as the oxen he uses to plow the fields."

She shook her head. "That's not what I'm thinking about."

He furrowed his brow in confusion. And then it dawned on him. On the day of the accident that had taken her *bruder*'s life and left her injured, the ambulance had brought her to this very hospital.

"Lizzie. I'll be by your side the whole time. I promise," Paul said.

"The last time I was in this building was all those years ago. I don't remember everything. Just…there was so much blood." She started to pull away.

* * *

She felt Paul place his hand under her elbow. For a brief moment Lizzie allowed herself to take comfort from his touch. It would be so easy to let him take the lead, but Lizzie wanted to be strong for her family. As they made their way down a long hallway, she tried hard to ignore the antiseptic smell. The acrid scent brought to mind what little she remembered about that long-ago day. She covered the scar on her face with a hand, feeling the soft ridge of skin, remembering the blood.

Lizzie jumped as the sound of Paul's voice jarred her back to the present.

"Here we are." He looked down at her and then nodded in the direction of the emergency room.

Lizzie appreciated the concern in his eyes, even though it did little to calm her nerves.

"Are you going to be okay?"

She dropped her hand against her side, nodding. Lizzie walked with him through another set of sliding glass doors and looked around the brightly lit area. It wasn't long before she saw her *mamm*'s plain black shoes poking out from beneath a curtained-off section of the large room. Heading that way, Lizzie slowly pulled back the white curtain and peeked in. Her *vader* lay on a narrow bed, with wires coming out from beneath a white blanket that covered him. His eyes were closed and his face looked very pale. Thankfully his chest rose and fell in a regular rhythm. Her gaze followed the cords to a monitor on a pole.

She heard the beeping of his heart and saw a wavy line running across the flat screen.

"*Dochder.* You shouldn't be here." Her father's weak voice startled her.

Lizzie stepped into the tiny space, while her *mamm* stood to gather her in a hug. "It's going to be all right," she whispered against Lizzie's ear.

"I'm worried about you, *Vader.*"

"I'm..." He paused, struggling to take a deep breath. "I'm going to be out of here in time for the next milking."

Her *mamm* gasped. "No, Joseph. That is *not* what the doctor said."

"What did they say, *mamm*?" Lizzie wanted to know.

"They could tell from the EKG that they ran in the ambulance that he's had a mild heart attack. He needs to stay here for a few more days while they run some more tests. They want to do a procedure called a catheterization to see if there is any damage to your *vader*'s heart."

"I won't be here for any of that," her *vader* grumbled. "I am in the middle of the first harvest. It's not like I have a strong son who can take over."

Lizzie stiffened at her father's harsh words. She knew better than he what the family had lost. Even though he'd never come out and accused her, she knew he blamed her for David's death. She felt her *mamm* give her hand a quick squeeze.

She released Lizzie, then walked across the polished black-and-white floor tiles to her husband's bedside. She took his hand in hers and kissed the top of it.

Very quietly, but with a firmness in her tone, she said, "Joseph, you will do exactly as the doctors tell you."

"But who will take care of the cows and the crops?"

Paul and a tall man dressed in Plain clothes entered their room. Lizzie recognized Amos Yoder, one of the elders in their church district. He stood at the foot of her father's bed, wearing dark pants and a crisp white shirt tucked beneath his black suspenders. On his head he wore a dark brimmed hat with a black band.

"Joseph," he said, his deep voice resonating throughout the space. "You will not worry about your crops or your cows. The men and I can each spare a son to help out until you are well enough. The boys will rotate their days."

Her *vader* sighed. He avoided making eye contact with her. "See, this mess has already brought the two of you away from your work."

"It was nothing, Joseph. I was at the house, visiting already, and didn't mind coming with Lizzie to the hospital," Paul said.

Taking her *mamm* aside, Lizzie knew she and Paul had stayed past their time. And she didn't want to be the cause of any more stress for her *vader*.

"*Mamm*, I think I'll go home. I've kept Paul here long enough, and I have much to tend to back at the house."

"*Ja*, Lizzie, you go home. If there are men working at our fields and in our barns, they will eventually need to be fed. You must cook for them."

"*Ja.* Of course." Her *mamm* led her back to her *vader*'s bedside so she could say goodbye. "*Vader*, I don't want you to worry about the farm. I can help keep things running." Lizzie tried her best to put on a brave front. But the truth was she was worried.

"Ach!" Her *vader* half raised a hand off the bed, swishing it in the air as if swatting at a fly. "You go home and do your chores, *Dochder*. I'll be fine."

Though she wanted with all her heart to believe him, she couldn't be certain how much damage his heart had sustained. Lizzie bent to kiss him on the cheek, but he turned his head, avoiding her touch. Fighting back the tears, she simply patted him on the shoulder and left the emergency room. She walked back down the long corridor with Paul. The stale antiseptic smells receded with each step she took. Lizzie made it to the main waiting room and exhaled.

She turned to Paul and said, "Take me home, please."

They stepped out of the sterile air of the hospital into the fresh air and fading sunlight of another hot summer day. Lizzie stood looking at the golden light, thankful to God above that her *vader* had survived. While she waited, Paul found them a cab to take them home.

Lizzie settled into the back seat, relieved to be going home. Paul got in and sat next to her. The car was small, and their shoulders bumped. Lizzie could feel the warmth coming from Paul's body. He'd been so kind to her today. But she couldn't allow him to be away from his own work. They both needed to get back to Miller's Crossing. She couldn't bear to be away from home for too long; even the short time away today left her feeling uneasy. She worried about what she was going to find when she got back to the farm. There was livestock to be fed and cows to be milked. She had no idea where her *vader* had left the tractor or who was going to see to the remainder of the cutting in the field he'd been harvesting this morning.

Lizzie felt the uncertainty creeping in like fog on a cool morning. She tried with all her might to bolster her confidence, thinking she could do this for her father. She owed him all the help she could give him. She could run things while he was in the hospital, couldn't she? Lizzy breathed a sigh of relief as the cab turned onto the road that led to the Miller farm.

And then she gasped in surprise at the sight that greeted her.

Chapter Two

From across the field that separated the property from the road, Lizzie could see a row of buggies parked in front of the barn.

"Oh, my, Paul! Look at all of this!"

He tilted his head toward her and smiled, nodding toward the house. "I told you, as soon as they heard about your *vader*, everyone came to help."

As the taxi pulled into the driveway, Lizzie pressed her forehead against the passenger-side window to get a better view of the yard. She saw her best friend, Sadie Fischer, rushing toward them. Immediately Lizzie's heart swelled with emotion. She didn't know what she would do without her friend. Waiting for the cab to stop, Lizzie tore off her seat belt and opened the door, stepping straight into her friend's outstretched arms.

"Lizzie, I'm so sorry to hear about your *vader*."

"Danke," Lizzie mumbled against Sadie's shoulder.

After releasing her hold, Lizzie looked around,

taking stock of the busy yard. Behind her she heard Paul paying the cab driver. She noted the crunch of the gravel as the car drove off. Paul came to stand near them.

"Is it true that your *vader* had a heart attack?" Sadie asked, her gaze darting from Paul to Lizzie.

"*Ja*. We think he's going to be fine, though," she answered, crossing her arms over her stomach as the full impact of her *vader*'s condition hit her.

With her sister, Mary, living in her husband's community in Montgomery County, a few hours from here, it was up to Lizzie to keep things running on the farm until her *mamm* or *vader* returned home.

Sadie quickly picked up on her unease. Her friend patted her on the arm, saying, "All will be well in time. Already we are all praying for his speedy recovery." Pointing toward the side yard, Sadie added, "See there? Those people are your friends and they care a great deal about your *vader*."

Lizzie looked past Sadie and saw a group of her neighbors and other community members standing in a circle, their heads bowed. The hems on the women's blue dresses flapped against their legs as a warm summer breeze blew across the yard. Some of the men had left their jobs to come and offer support. Even though she knew it was the way of the Amish to come and lend a helping hand to a neighbor in need, she still felt uneasy about having all these people at her home. It appeared, though, that Sadie and Paul were both correct: everyone was doing something to help.

Her lower lip trembled as she fought back her

tears. "*Vader* sent me back. He said there was a lot that needed to be tended to. And it looks like he was right." Lizzie swiped a hand across her cheeks, starting to walk toward the house.

Paul fell into step beside them. "I see my *bruders*, Ben and Abram are here."

He nodded in the direction of the barn, where Lizzie could see fourteen-year-old Abram walking out of the barn with a wheelbarrow full of horse manure. Ben came out behind him, yelling that Abram had left a mess behind.

"So, three Burkholders have set aside their own chores for my family," Lizzie mumbled, nodding at them. They gave her a wave, and then she dipped her head to one side. "That was very kind of them to come by."

A monarch butterfly flitted in front of her face. Lizzie raised her hand, swishing it away, not in the mood to ponder the creature.

"I need to get to the kitchen. I understand there are men out in the field, working to bring in the rest of the hay that *Vader* was harvesting this morning. And then there are the cows to milk and feed. I'll need to cook something to feed everyone." She twisted her mouth into a thin line, making a mental list of the food they had on hand.

She knew there would be enough chicken for a stew, and there were several loaves of bread in the pantry, along with beans and potatoes. There were some zucchini squash, tomatoes, cucumbers and lettuce in the garden that could be picked.

Paul caught her gaze and smiled. "Listen to me. You have plenty of help everywhere, even in the kitchen. I suspect my *mamm* is here, too."

"What? I can't have your whole family at our house."

"Trust me, I have plenty of family to go around." He let out a chuckle. "With my five siblings, the lot of them would easily fill up your kitchen."

She managed to muster a smile.

He gently walked her and Sadie down the drive, up the porch steps and into the house, where a beehive of activity was going on. Excusing herself, Sadie rushed into the kitchen, making her way over to the long counter. Lizzie watched her laying out rows of sliced white bread. To her right another young woman was adding slices of cheese and turkey to one side of the sandwich. Paul had left her to go say hello to his *mamm*, who was dumping boiled potatoes from a large pot into a colander in the sink.

Lizzie realized she'd been standing in the doorway. Looking down at her apron, the same light blue color as her dress, Lizzie frowned. Despite her fatigue, with her *mamm* absent it was her duty to help run things in the kitchen. Pulling the apron she'd been wearing over her shoulders, she shrugged out of it. She hung it on one of the wall pegs near the front door. Her hand brushed against a boy's straw hat. The felt band looked brand-new. But Lizzie knew it was exactly ten years old.

Some days she wished her *mamm* would put the hat away. Seeing that hat reminded everyone of David.

She put her house apron on and tied the sash around her waist. Having the hat here or not, Lizzie would never forget her *bruder*. Unlike in the homes of their *Englisch* neighbors, here there were no family photos, so they were left with only the memory of the images of their lives.

Lizzie closed her eyes, seeing David's face in her mind's eye. The eyes that matched hers in color, the dark hair that no matter how hard *Mamm* tried to brush it in place, always stuck out from beneath this hat. She imagined the dimples that appeared when he smiled. She heard his laughter. She shook her head to clear out those thoughts. Blinking away the emotions that seemed to come every time she thought of her *bruder*, Lizzie realized Sadie had stopped making sandwiches and was watching her with concern.

Crossing the room, she came over to her. "How about you let me get you a nice glass of the fresh lemonade that Mrs. Yoder brought over."

"That would be nice," Lizzie said as she took another apron from a peg and put it on. Tying the sash off, she followed Sadie into the kitchen.

Lizzie took the glass from her friend's hand, not realizing until this moment how thirsty she was. She took a gulp from the drink, letting the coolness slide down her parched throat. She set the half-empty glass on the counter, wondering where to begin. At the back of the kitchen, a door stood ajar. If not for her *vader*'s health, the laundry room would have been bustling with activity today.

Not only were the long summer days good for

bringing in the hay, but they were also good for drying the wash. All through their community, backyard clotheslines would be filled with dark pants, white shirts and dresses. Monday was wash day. And the cars would come through in slow, long lines as the tourists tried to capture the image of their laundry on their fancy cameras or cell phones. Lizzie wanted to laugh because if they knew how much work was involved in getting a single load of wash done, maybe they'd see those images in a different way.

The dark pants, blue shirts, dresses and aprons would have to wait until tomorrow for their washing because right now there was a group of men waiting to be fed. Lizzie began helping the women carry out the bowls of potato salad and fruit salad, along with the platter of sandwiches and cutlery to a makeshift plywood-and-sawhorse table that had been set up underneath the shade of a large maple tree out in the backyard.

One of the women had gone to signal to the men that it was mealtime. She heard the clanking of the bell that hung outside the front door. In some homes a bell like this would be used to signal an emergency. Her father had installed a phone shanty on their property a few years ago. It was only used for business or for emergencies. Today she'd been beyond thankful for the convenience. Though it had seemed like an hour to her, the ambulance had arrived within minutes of her 911 call.

She knew in some Amish communities, the *Ordnung* forbade the use of any kind of phones, in which case a person had to travel to the nearest business to use one or depend on their *Englisch* neighbors to let them borrow theirs. Lizzie had even heard of some of the younger folks being allowed the use of cell phones. She shook her head at that thought. She couldn't imagine needing one of those.

Here in Miller's Crossing, New York, there were several Amish communities. The one where her family lived was allowed to have curtains on their windows and linoleum flooring in the houses. Lizzie felt pleased to have some of the more modern amenities. This brought her sister, Mary, to mind. As soon as the meal was over, she would get a message to her about their *vader*. Her sister had married Aaron Yoder last year and moved over an hour away. Mary and Aaron's church *Ordnung* didn't allow for such niceties in the homes. It had been a week or so since Mary's last letter. Lizzie knew her *schweschder* had had some trouble adjusting to her new life, but she loved her husband, so she was willing to try. The family was planning to be together the first Tuesday in October for their cousin Rachel's wedding.

Thoughts of Mary's new life and their cousin's wedding gave Lizzie pause. With her *vader*'s heart condition, she had no idea what tomorrow would hold, let alone if they could actually attend the wedding. As she spooned potato salad onto the plates, she thought about how all around her, family and friends were starting new lives, growing their own families. And here she was, still on the farm with her *mamm* and *vader* like a *bobbli*. Yes, she loved her life here, even if at times things did seem complicated. Even before his sudden illness, her *vader* had needed help on the farm. If she were to take a husband, things could be different.

As she so often found herself doing in times of stress, Lizzie ran her hand along the scar on her face. What man would want someone so disfigured? Out of the corner of her eye, she watched Paul acting kind with his *mamm*. Lizzie couldn't help but think of all the years of kindness he'd shown her. He was a good friend and neighbor. A fine man. Paul would make an excellent husband for one lucky woman.

But that woman would not be her.

Paul had spotted his *mamm* at the stove in the Millers' kitchen, getting ready to drain a large pot of green beans into a colander in the sink, and hurried over to take the heavy pot from her.

"Here, *Mamm*. Let me do this for you."

"*Ja*, my strong son to the rescue," she said, stepping aside to let him dump the pot. The hot steam wafted up between them as the string beans and water fell into the metal colander. Gently nudging him aside, she took the colander from him and shook the vegetables from side to side, helping the water drain out.

"I see you brought Lizzie home from the hospital. She looks tired and worried," his mother said in a soft voice.

"The doctors haven't told them much about her *vader*'s heart condition. From the sounds of it, he'll be in the hospital a few more days while they run some tests."

"*Danke Gott* you were there when it happened."

Leaning his hip against the counter, Paul wondered about the cause of Mr. Miller's heart attack. Then again, from what he'd heard, these health conditions generally did not manifest overnight. Still, he imagined the stress of trying to run this farm singlehandedly hadn't helped. There had been rumors floating about in the community for a long time that the man had been working long hours, burning the candle at both ends, with not much help. Keeping that sort of pace for too long couldn't be good. Even though he generally worked long hours, Paul always left time in his week for time off to pray and reflect. As he recalled, Joseph Miller had been absent from the past few church meetings. A habit that was highly frowned upon by the church leaders.

"I'm not sure I did anything that mattered other than check to see if he was breathing."

His *mamm* patted him on the arm, saying, "You were there for Lizzie. And you made sure she got to and from the hospital. That's what's important, *sohn*. That's what she'll remember."

"I'm her friend—of course I was there for her."

He stopped thinking about Lizzie for a moment and then wondered what his *mamm* would do when she found out what his plans for the future were. Though he knew she wanted the best for him, he also didn't want to be the cause of conflict in the family.

"Paul..."

The sound of her quiet voice brought him out of his reverie. From the soft look on her face, he knew exactly what she was going to say about the relationship between him and Lizzie.

Paul cut her off with, "Please don't go there. To me, she's always been and will always be David's sister. Nothing more."

She gave him a thoughtful look, her brown eyes warm with love and bracketed with fine lines. She patted him on the arm, then said, "If that's how you want to see it. One more thing to consider, my *sohn*, that tragic day happened a long time ago. I know sometimes it's hard to understand *Gott*'s ways. But you and Lizzie, you need to make peace and put the past where it belongs. Your future could be bright."

"I'm friends with her. Nothing more," he insisted.

As she turned away from him to put the string beans in a large bowl, he heard her mumble, "For now."

Chapter Three

Taking the bowl from his *mudder*, he dropped a kiss on her cheek and then headed out to the backyard. He walked over to the food table and handed the bowl to Lizzie. She barely gave him any attention as she took the beans from him.

"I'll take that bowl off your hands," she said.

He tipped his hat to her and went to find a seat at the makeshift table.

While he dug into the midday meal, he became aware of Lizzy's gaze on him. He wondered what she was thinking. No doubt she was still feeling overwhelmed at finding herself in charge of the household for the moment. He gave her a smile, knowing that even if she didn't think so, she was more than capable of handling the situation.

He shuffled down a few spaces on the bench as his *bruder* Abram plunked his plate down and swung a leg over to sit beside him. Paul watched in awe as he emptied the plate of the large portion of potato salad in three forkfuls.

"You need to slow down, Abram, or one of these days you'll end up choking."

His brother smiled at him and shook his head, saying, "*Mamm*'s salad is still the best in these parts."

Paul nodded as he picked up the sandwich he'd added to his plate. Taking a generous bite, he realized he was hungry, too. He also realized he needed to get back home to do the chores there and help finish up the cabinet job he had been helping his *vader* with. Swallowing, he knew he had to talk to his *vader* soon. The man who owned the building Paul was interested in renting wanted to know how soon he could begin leasing it.

It was a good price and he didn't want to lose the opportunity to set up his own store there. It was a great location, only half a block up from the main intersection in the village. Paul knew the tourists would come into the store. They loved to buy Amish goods. He felt if he listed his furniture at a good but fair price that he would do well.

After finishing his meal, he took his plate over to the makeshift washing area that had been set up outside the kitchen. Leaving his plate there, he caught Lizzie's attention and waved at her. She gave him a half wave back. He walked around to the front of the Millers' house. As he made his way up the driveway, he looked off into the fields. He saw a wagon bringing in a load of hay bales. Near the barn, a line of cows with their udders full lumbered toward the milking parlor. All around him the air was filled with the earthy scents of the farm.

Ben met him halfway down the drive. As he came closer, Paul saw that he looked to be a bit concerned. Maybe there was a problem on the Millers' farm or he'd heard news about Lizzie's father. Either way he wasn't going to have to wait long to find out, because his *bruder* caught him by the arm and pulled him to the edge of the lawn.

"I was just up at our house and *Daed* is upset with some news he heard from the owner of the general store. Is it true you've been looking into renting some shop space?"

A knot formed in the pit of his stomach as he met his brother's firm gaze. He'd hoped that word of his plans would not be spread around yet. But small towns being what they were, the thought that he'd be the one to deliver the news to his *vader* the way he saw fit had been ridiculous to begin with. Frowning at his brother, who'd grown so much over the past spring that he now stood eye to eye with him, Paul knew his *vader* had to be angry about this.

The Burkholders had been living in Miller's Crossing since their Amish community had been founded back in the 1950s by Lizzie's great-grandfather, Levi Miller. The group had traveled from Ohio in search of affordable farmland and had come upon this vast area of Chautauqua County. Over time, due to the changing economy, the farms had shrunk and the members of the community had taken to establishing lumberyards and other small but sustainable businesses.

Paul's father had served at one time as the head of their church. Now he was busy with the family furniture business. Though he knew his father would stay tied to their property, Paul wanted desperately to have his own business in the village. He was in his twenties now and wanted to be making his own way within Miller's Crossing.

"Paul, is it true?" Ben asked again.

"Yes," Paul answered as he looked at the deepening crease on his brother's forehead. Of all his siblings, Ben was the one who worried the most.

Continuing up the hill to the top of the driveway, Paul clasped his hand against his brother's back. "You let me deal with our *daed*."

"He doesn't want you to leave."

Paul shook his head. "I'm not leaving the family. I'm only going into town to sell my furniture."

"Plenty of *Englischers* stop by our shop," Ben said.

"They do. But we could be doing better."

"We are doing okay. There's always food on the table and warmth in the house." Ben's face turned red as he argued his point.

Paul didn't respond to his *bruder*, other than mentioning the fact that he wanted his own business. He enjoyed working with wood. Smelling the shavings from the floor in the saw room and working to build fine furniture brought him great joy. More importantly, he liked to work with his hands.

He wasn't moving out of their farmhouse; he was simply making his own way in the community, like any *youngie* who was old enough to do so.

"We should be getting home."

"Ja." Paul walked over to where his brother had parked the wagon, climbed up and sat alongside him on the bench.

Paul picked up the reins and slapped them against the horse's backside. The wagon jumped forward as the horse picked up its pace. On the short ride home, Paul thought about what he was going to say to his *vader*. Paul knew he wasn't going to be able to change his *vader*'s ways, but he also knew deep in his heart that he wouldn't be changing his mind, either. He nudged the horse to the right, making a wide turn with the wagon onto the dirt road that led to his family's ninety-acre parcel. Most of the land was covered in trees, which were eventually cut into lumber and used in their furniture business. As he drove past their family's large white farmhouse, he gave a tug on the leather straps of the reins, signaling for the horse to turn onto a narrow dirt roadway that allowed access to their barn. Up ahead stood the attached structure of the woodworking shop, where he and his *bruders* worked alongside their *vader*.

Knowing the path well, the horse came to a stop right in front of the open side door. Paul set the reins on the seat between him and Ben. He could feel his *bruder*'s gaze on him. The last thing on this earth that he would ever do would be to hurt his family. He prayed that his *vader* would see his reasons for wanting to open up his own shop.

He felt Ben's hand on his arm.

"I'll see to the horses. You go on inside," Ben said, still looking worried.

Paul jumped down from the wagon and ducked inside the doorway of the spacious workshop.

"Hallo! Is anybody here?" Paul strode through the large open area, where neat piles of lumber stood stacked shoulder height on top of a row of pallets.

"*Ja.* What's all this shouting?" His vader came out of the workshop, shaking the wood shavings off his leather apron.

Paul looked at the man who, if not for the slight hunch in his back, would be the exact same height as himself. "I've got things squared away over at the Miller house," he said, looking into eyes that were the same shade as his.

They also shared the same square jawline and cleft chin. Besides their age, their one big difference was the gray hair sprinkled throughout his *vader*'s beard.

"How is Joseph doing?"

"As far as I know, he's going to be in the hospital for a few more days while they run some tests."

His *vader* didn't say anything for a few minutes. Paul knew to wait for him to speak.

His *vader* nodded to the stack of wood slabs to the right of Paul, saying, "Help me bring two more of these inside."

Hoisting one end of the slab onto his shoulder, *vader* said, "Seems like there was a lot of excitement at the Miller house today. It will be some time before things return to normal."

"*Ja*, for sure and certain. But Lizzie had a lot of

help today. And for many days to come, if her family needs it, no doubt."

"That's good."

Paul took the other end and followed him into the workroom. They set the wood on top of a large counter. On the wall at the back of the area was a large pegboard where all of the tools hung in neat rows. They worked in silence for a bit while they prepared for the project his *vader* had been working on. Paul knew better than to try to coax any conversation out of the man. So he waited.

When his *vader* stopped to wipe his forehead with a handkerchief, Paul knew the time had come.

"I've a thermos of iced tea over there on the table. Why don't you pour us some?"

Doing as his *vader* had asked, Paul came back to hand his father a full cup, saying, "It looks like you've got the Smiths' cabinet order almost finished."

"*Ja*. This was an easy project. They only needed a simple cupboard for their little girl's bedroom." His father said, then took a sip from the cup. He took his time drinking the cool liquid.

Paul found he wasn't all that thirsty.

"I heard from the owner of Becker's grocery that you've been asking around about renting shop space in the village. Did he speak the truth?"

Paul met his *vader*'s hard stare. Even though he'd known this time had come, it didn't make standing here any easier. "*Ja*, he did."

"You're going to leave your family?" His face reddened.

"I am *not* leaving the family."

"That is what it sounds like to me, *sohn*."

"*Daed.* I've been looking at our sales numbers for the past few years and we could be doing better."

"We are doing well enough."

Paul sighed. "I want to put my furniture out where it will be seen by the tourists who are traveling through."

"We get plenty of them right now. Besides, I need you here to help with the farm chores."

Like most of the community, the Burkholders had both their farm and a business. Some families specialized in cheese production, others canned goods and bakery items. The Troyers had a very popular greenhouse business four miles from here. The Burkholders were cabinetmakers and furniture makers.

"I can still be doing my chores here and working on the family business." He knew he had to tread lightly, but in his heart, Paul also knew moving his side of the business was where his future lay. Expanding into the village would eventually bring the entire family more revenue. Paul wanted to make this work. "I would like to be able to do this with your blessing."

"You should be concentrating on finding a wife." *Vader* wagged his finger at him. "You get married, have children and then you can think about this business idea. Right now your place is here, helping me keep your *bruders* in line, seeing to the daily chores and working here—" he paused to spread his hands wide "—with your family."

Paul lowered his gaze to stare at the top of his boots. He wanted to give his *vader* time to think about the possibility of expanding, and yet if he didn't act soon, the shop would surely be rented out to someone else. He couldn't let that happen.

"You need time to think about this," Paul said in a quiet voice.

"*Nee*, I don't. Your place is here." His *vader*'s tone was dismissive. "Another order for a cabinet came in while you were over at the Millers'. I wrote the dimensions down. You can get started on that."

Paul loved and respected his *vader*, but he couldn't accept his decision. Not when Paul hadn't even shown him his plans for the new store, or explained to him how this would help the entire Burkholder family, not just himself. But his father had turned his back on him. The last time he'd wanted to go against his *vader*'s wishes had been the day David Miller had died.

Paul had wanted to go play with his friends in the barn, but it had been a particularly trying day at their house with the loss of one of their cows after a difficult birth. Paul remembered wanting to be allowed to play. That day he'd followed his father's wishes and stayed home. The outcome had left one friend dead and one scarred for life. To this day he'd felt that if he could have been there in that barn with his childhood friends, he could have prevented what had happened. Paul had never forgiven himself for what had happened.

Now, more than ever, he wanted to stand his ground. He wanted to see his dream of one day having his own store become a reality. He knew about the pride the Amish took in their families and their homes; after all he had the same pride. He'd taken his time when it'd been his turn to partake in *rumspringa*. Then Paul had thought about his life as an Amish man, the only life he'd ever known, and how he wanted to be a part of this church district. It had been seven years since he'd taken his vow and been baptized into the church.

He didn't see how taking the furniture business into town meant he wouldn't still be a part of his family's life here. His plan had always been to live here and work in the village. He had to find a way to make his father come around and give him his blessing. There would be plenty of time later to think about taking a wife and making his own home. He closed his eyes, and for the briefest moment pictured Lizzie standing by his side.

He knew that dream was further away from reality than owning his own business was.

Lizzie sat in her *vader*'s favorite chair, the one that had soft fabric covering plump cushions, and looked out the front window. It had been a very long day and she should have been sound asleep in her bed. But her mind wouldn't settle. There were too many thoughts and memories from this day swirling around in her head. Her *mamm* had sent a message saying she would be staying at the hospital with her *vader* overnight. Sadie had offered to stay over so Lizzie wasn't alone in the house, but Lizzie had sent her home. Lizzie didn't mind having some quiet time to herself.

Resting her elbows on the chair arms, she looked

out the window and up into the night sky. There had to be a million stars shimmering against the inky blackness. The moon was three-quarters full and cast a sharp glow over the landscape. She looked out over the yard, where the tree limbs swayed in the breeze, their shadows dancing over the dewy lawn. Behind her the clock on the mantel in the living room showed it was ten o'clock.

Lizzie curled her hand into a soft fist and tucked it beneath her chin. She sat for a few more moments, pondering the day. She thought about how kind Paul had been to her; from the moment he'd brought her the paints until the time he'd returned home, she'd felt his kindness. Lizzie wasn't sure she deserved it. For years she'd been pushing him away. Though she appreciated his friendship, there could never be anything more between them. Even the things they wanted in life were so different.

Paul wanted to open up a shop in the village. She didn't understand how he could walk away from his family business. He'd begun to tell her about it earlier today, but they were interrupted by the hospital receptionist. Lizzie was content to stay home with her parents and help run the household. He liked talking to strangers and making them beautiful furniture for their homes. She wasn't comfortable being around people she didn't know. Even on the days when she had to go to the village to shop for her *mamm*, she timed it so there would be hardly any crowds in the stores. Lizzie imagined she could be content to stay just as she was. And now, with her *vader*'s illness, she was needed here more than ever. And when she needed a break, she could go off with her sketch pad and draw.

Off in the distance she heard the sound of a cow mooing. Lizzie looked out toward the barn. She saw a tall figure holding a lantern high.

Her heart pounded inside her chest, and then the man turned to look up at the house. *Paul.* Relief flooded through her as she stood up and went to open the front door. She stepped out onto the porch and waited for him to approach.

"Good evening, Lizzie."

"You gave me quite a fright, you know," Lizzie scolded him from the top of the porch step.

"I'm sorry. I wanted to make sure the cows were secure."

"That's very kind of you," she replied, putting her hand to her mouth to stifle a yawn. "Oh, my. I'm so sorry. I don't mean to be yawning at you." A nervous laugh escaped her.

Still holding the lantern out in one hand, he shoved the other into the side pocket of his dark pants. "Don't worry. I know you've had a very long day. Has there been any word on your *vader*?"

"*Nee.* My *mamm* is staying at the hospital with him tonight."

Through the darkness he studied her, as if trying to decide if it were safe for her to remain here alone.

Finally he said, "Promise me you will lock the doors."

"I will. *Danke* again for everything you've done."

"It was no trouble. I'll be back tomorrow to take a shift with the chores."

"Good night, Paul."

"Good night, Lizzie."

He turned and walked back down the pathway. She watched him until he was nothing more than a shadow in the fading moonlight. Long after Paul had gone, she stared at the barn doors. So many terrible memories of this day lingered inside that building.

She stepped back inside the house and shut the front door, locking it behind her. Turning around she spotted the bag Paul had given her lying on the side table, where she'd left it this morning. She nibbled on her lower lip, contemplating what was inside. Colors. He'd told her she should add colors to her drawings. It was easy to imagine tufts of green grass and swaths of blue sky coming to life on the paper.

After going into her bedroom and opening the bottom drawer in the dresser, she took out her sketch pad and pencils. Then she came back into the living room, sat down, turned up the lamp and then flipped the pad open to the last drawing she'd been working on. The bare-bones image of the barn glared up at her. Her heart felt as if it were squeezing inside her chest as she looked at the plain lines she'd drawn a few weeks ago. Lizzie picked up the pencil and held it poised over the page. Maybe Paul was right. She needed to bring color to her work, and to her life, she thought. Perhaps only then could she erase the starkness of the memories that haunted her.

Sighing, she set the pencil down and closed her

sketchbook. It had been a long, long day. Shaking her head, Lizzie mused. Nothing about the past could be changed. Nothing. She needed to stop dwelling on what might have been. Being here with her parents, staying within the close comfort of the farm, this was her life. There was nothing for her beyond the fences.

It was time she accepted that and put thoughts of love and family out of her mind. For good.

Chapter Four

The white sheets snapped in the warm breeze. Lizzie stood on tiptoe, attaching the last sheet to the line that ran from their back door clear up to the top of the old pine tree that stood in the middle of the yard. It had been a long week. Her father had finally come home from the hospital after a five-day stay. They had put something called a stent in to open up the damaged artery. Lizzie had been more than grateful for the community that had come out to support them.

Paul's *mudder* had stepped in to coordinate the kitchen help, making sure that there was plenty of food to feed the helpers. There had been a never-ending supply of Mrs. Burkholder's potato salad. The refrigerator still held some of those leftovers. As promised, each of the men had sent over *sohns* to help out with the feedings, in addition to finishing up the plowing and haying her *vader* had begun the day of his heart attack. As was the Amish way in times of need, her neighbors had been very generous with their time and resources. Lizzie hoped that one day she could repay them in kind.

As she hung the last sheet on the line, clamping the wooden clothespin into place, Lizzie took a deep breath. Inhaling the sweet summer breeze, laced with the earthy scent of the freshly mowed alfalfa fields and the fully blooming pink rose bushes growing beside the back stoop, made her feel alive and grateful to live in such a beautiful place. Even with the steep and sometimes treacherous hills that surrounded Miller's Crossing, making it difficult to get around during the winter, Lizzie found comfort by simply being here, in this moment.

Since the return home of her father and seeing how wan he still looked, she knew it might be days before their life returned to normal. This morning he and her *mamm* had been driven to a follow-up doctor's appointment by their neighbor, Helen Meyers. Lizzie didn't know what they would have done without her. From the very beginning she'd been kind enough to offer up her services for any errands and appointments that her family needed a car for.

And right now there were a half-dozen men working out in the field and loading the hay wagons with freshly cut silage. The motor of the blower for the silo had been running for two days straight.

She paused on the porch step. Putting her hand above her forehead to shield the bright sunlight from her eyes, she looked out over the lawn to the closest field. She scanned the horizon, seeing a low wagon loaded with jugs of lemonade, water and red coolers.

She turned her attention to the workers, not wanting to admit that she was searching for someone in particular. It wasn't long before she spotted Paul. He stood tall, his straw hat in one hand, while he wiped a white cloth over his face with the other. He had the sleeves of his blue chambray shirt rolled up above the elbows.

He turned then and saw her watching him. His mouth tilted up as he gave a slight nod. Embarrassed that she'd been caught gawking, Lizzie scurried into the coolness of the house. Today she was going to be baking up a batch of cookies for the men to enjoy on their afternoon break.

Once in the kitchen she turned on the oven, setting the temperature to preheat to 350 degrees. Then she began to gather the ingredients for her favorite cookies. She took the flour, white sugar, brown sugar and other dry ingredients from the pantry to the large farm table in the middle of the kitchen. The cookies she'd chosen to make today were called Double-Treat Cookies. The recipe called for peanut butter, salted peanuts and semisweet chocolate chips. She'd made them countless times over the years for gatherings. And never once had there been leftovers.

While searching for the butter, she realized that Paul had been here every day since her *vader*'s heart attack. It troubled her that he'd neglected his own work to be here. Blowing out a frustrated breath, she kept looking for those sticks of butter in the refrigerator that she knew were there somewhere. Turning around, she walked over to the stove and saw that the butter was sitting on the counter, right where she'd left it yesterday after baking buttermilk biscuits for their supper.

She picked it up and went back to the refrigerator, opened the door and took two eggs from the wire egg basket. Seeing the mound of eggs reminded her that she still needed to fill the cartons to take down to her roadside stand. She would tend to that after the cookies were baked. There simply weren't enough hours in the day to get everything done. She set to work sifting together the flour, baking soda and salt in a medium-sized bowl. Then, picking up the hand mixer, she combined the shortening, sugars, eggs and a generous teaspoon of vanilla in a large bowl until everything was light and fluffy. Looking around the table, she realized she'd forgotten to bring over the jar of peanut butter.

Lizzie had her head stuck in the pantry once again when she heard a knock on the front door. Quickly she grabbed the jar and hurried to see who was there. With the jar still in hand, she looked through the screen door to find Paul standing on the other side. His face was flushed from the heat. There were a few smudges of dirt on his otherwise neatly tucked-in shirt.

"Good morning, Lizzie." Paul tipped his hat to her.

She took a step back into the shadows, nodding at him. "Hello, Paul."

"May I come inside?" he asked with a gentle half smile.

She only now noticed he'd been holding an empty jug in his hands.

He stepped aside as she pushed the door open, allowing him to come into the house.

"I'm busy baking cookies."

He followed her into the kitchen. "I won't take up too much of your time—I promise. I came to get a refill of the lemonade."

"You can help yourself to the container in the refrigerator."

He set the jug down and washed his hands in the sink before he went to get the refill.

Lizzie set the peanut butter on the table and found that her hands were shaking as she unscrewed the lid, which seemed to be stuck.

"Here, let me help." He took the jar from her hands.

Paul's touch felt warm. Lizzie quickly removed her hands from the jar, clasping them in front of her. She watched him open the lid with one strong twist. Wasn't that always the way, she thought, a woman would work hard to get something unscrewed and then a man would come along and make it look easy as pie.

"You must've loosened the jar," he said as he winked at her, handing the jar back. "What are you making today?"

"My Double-Treat Cookies."

"You made them for the last frolic. They were good."

"Danke."

Silence descended on them. For a moment Lizzie

thought Paul was going to take his lemonade and leave; instead he pulled up a stool from beneath the table and sat. He then folded his arms in front of him and rested them on the tabletop. Unsure of what to do, she offered him a glass of lemonade. Which seemed silly, considering he'd just filled up an entire jug with the sweet liquid. When he accepted, she busied herself with pouring him a glass.

Setting it before him, she said, "If you don't mind, I need to keep mixing the dough so I can have the cookies ready for the workers' next break." She thought he might leave then, but he only nodded, took a healthy gulp out of the glass, set it down and looked like he would be settling in for a bit.

Setting to work getting the dry ingredients mixed with the wet, Lizzie tried not to think about the fact that Paul was watching her every move. She knew he must have his own work to do and wondered why he was still here. She began to roll the dough into teaspoon-sized balls. Each one was rolled in a bowl of granulated sugar, and then after that was done, she spaced them apart on the cookie sheet.

She was flattening the dough balls with the bottom of a drinking glass when Paul said, "You're mighty good at baking, Lizzie."

"You haven't even tasted these yet, so how do you know how good they are?"

"I remember how they tasted the last time you made them. You haven't changed the recipe, have you?"

"Nee." Turning her back to him, she walked over

to the oven and placed the first cookie sheet on the baking rack. Then she set the oven timer for seven minutes, even though the recipe called for eight minutes of cooking time. Sometimes the oven could be finicky. She didn't want the cookies to burn on the bottom.

When she turned back to the table, she found Paul looking a bit contemplative, staring off into space. His behavior was very unusual. Why was he here? she wondered again. Was he here to deliver her bad news? Shaking that thought away, she continued to load a second tray of cookies. The sound of his voice broke into her thoughts.

"Give me the glass and let me flatten them."

Her motion stilled as she looked across the table at him, meeting his gaze head-on. Her stomach jittered with butterfly nerves. "Why on earth would you want to help me bake? This is a woman's job. Shouldn't you be getting back home or back out in the field?"

He crooked an eyebrow. "Are you anxious to be rid of me so fast?"

"Nee," she mumbled.

Taking the glass from the table, he pulled the tray closer to where he sat and began flattening the cookies with such intensity that Lizzie had to stop him.

"You don't need to hit them that hard, Paul. These are supposed to be plump cookies." She reached out to take the glass from him, except he held fast to it.

"I'm sorry. I'm having a bad day is all." Finally he handed the glass back to her. Frowning down at his hands, he shook his head. "I'm going to sign the lease papers for the shop in the village this week."

She pulled a stool out, sat opposite him and said, "This feels so sudden, and yet I know you've been thinking on this for a long time."

"Yes, I have. It's been consuming most of my thoughts. My *vader* is not happy about it. I've tried to speak with him, tried to get him to change his mind, but he won't budge. He thinks I'm going to somehow damage the family by doing this."

"I remember you started to tell me about this idea last week at the hospital. I'm sorry your *vader* feels this way."

He lifted his head and looked into her eyes. "I'm going to do this with or without his blessing."

Surprised by his determination, Lizzie didn't quite know what to say. "Paul, are you willing to put your family at risk for this choice?" She paused a moment, then went on. "I know how my own *vader* feels about keeping his family nearby. I imagine yours feels the same way about your staying on at the family business, keeping things the way they've been for years."

"Opening a second shop in the village will be good for everyone, Lizzie. More people will see the Burkholder name." He paused and then pointed out, "Your sister moved away and that changed your family."

"That was different. She moved away because her husband's family needed them more than we did." Lizzie realized it wasn't her place to tell Paul what to do.

Besides, who was she to give out advice? She kept

to herself here at the house. Lizzie had little idea about what living or working away from the family farm would be like. She only knew that her place was with her *mamm* and *vader*. Now more than ever she needed to be here, selling her eggs and baked goods to help keep her family going. Just like Paul, Lizzie had responsibilities that couldn't be ignored.

"The thing is, Lizzie, as I've told you before, I've been dreaming about a place of my own for some time now. And I'm not leaving the family or the farm. I'm simply moving my furniture business into the town so more tourists will see what we do out here. You know many of those *Englischers* are afraid to drive around these parts. I think when they get a glimpse of the steep rolling hills out this way, they get scared off."

"Paul, you must do what your *vader* asks of you."

"I don't know about that. My plan will help the family earn more money. He's afraid my brothers will run wild if I'm not around as much."

"You could always bring the oldest ones with you," Lizzie suggested.

"*Nee.* They need to be around to do the chores and help with the wood deliveries. And *Daed* needs their help loading up the cabinets if we have to deliver them. It's not a problem with the bigger pieces because most times those are ordered by outsiders and picked up by a freight truck."

The timer dinged, and Lizzie left the table to go check on the first batch of cookies. She took a pot holder and pulled out what looked to be a perfect batch from the oven and then placed the pan on the stovetop. The house was soon filled with the scent of warm sugar and peanut butter.

From behind her, Paul said, "Wow! Those smell delicious."

Taking a napkin from the basket on the counter, Lizzie placed one of the hot cookies on it and brought it back to the table. She set it in front of Paul. His eyes lit up.

The smile on his face broadened as he said, "Ah, my Lizzie, you do know the way to a hardworking man's heart."

She let out a gasp and stepped back. Out of a long-practiced instinct, her hand flew up to cover the scar on her face. She wasn't trying to work her way into anyone's heart, least of all Paul's. He was her childhood friend—nothing more. She could see the confusion over her actions dawning on his face.

He reached his hand out toward her, and then placed it on the table. "Lizzie." His tone softened. "I didn't mean to make you feel uncomfortable with my words. They were a compliment to your fine baking skills. Please don't shy away from me."

Slowly she lowered her hand.

"You don't need to hide your face from me ever. I need you to understand that, Lizzie."

She nodded slightly, fighting the urge to cover her scar again. Instead she busied herself by putting the next batch of cookies into the oven. Then picking up a spatula, she removed the baked ones to a wire rack, where they could cool the rest of the way. Bringing the sheet pan back to the table, she repeated the steps, getting the next dozen ready to be baked. All the while she felt his gaze on her. Finally she stopped and looked at him, instinct telling her where his thoughts were.

"Paul, there are things that happen in our lives, things that shape us…shape our future. My future is here, in this house, with my family." Her voice dropped to a notch above a whisper. "And as much as you want me to, I can't speak of that day. I just can't."

"There are things you don't know…" His voice trailed off. He turned his head, looking over his shoulder.

Lizzie had never been so thankful to hear the sound of the car doors slamming closed. Wiping her hand on her apron, she walked to the front door to meet her parents. Paul followed closely behind her. Pushing the screen door open, she walked out onto the porch.

"*Mamm! Daed!* I'm glad you're home." Lizzie rushed down the steps, coming alongside her parents. She thought her *daed* looked tired. It must have been a trying day traveling an hour to the hospital and then, no doubt, sitting in the waiting area for a bit.

"Lizzie, run into the house and get your *daed* some iced tea and a sandwich."

"Yes, *Mamm*," she said, hurrying back up the steps.

Stepping off the porch, Paul met Mr. Miller on the steps, saying, "Mr. and Mrs. Miller. I just came by to check in and to get a refill on this jug of lemonade." He held the container up.

"That was right kind of you, Paul. And we appreciate your being here to help, along with the others." Mrs. Miller smiled up at him.

He extended a hand to her husband, offering his help. "Here, let me get you up these steps."

Mr. Miller batted at his hand. "No need for assistance. I can get up there on my own."

The man put a shaky hand on the railing and pulled himself up the first step. Then, taking a deep breath, he moved up the last three steps and plunked himself down in the nearest rocking chair on the front porch. "There. I told you I could do this. Those doctors wanted me to go for physical therapy. They want me to walk on a treadmill. I told them I could take my walks in the outdoors, right here on my own property."

Looking kindly at the man, Paul could see where Lizzie's stubbornness came from. Mrs. Miller followed her husband onto the porch. Smiling at Mrs. Miller, he could see the resemblance between Lizzie and her mother. Mother and daughter carried the same blue eyes and dark hair. Though Lizzie's hair was touched by some honey-colored streaks.

From the rocker, Mr. Miller looked up at him. His cheeks carrying only a tinge of color, and his mouth a bit drawn. It appeared that the exertion of the day was catching up with him. Paul knew little about the man's heart condition, but he imagined recovering from a heart attack and surgery could knock the wind out of a body. When the man nodded to the rocker next to him, Paul started to go over to sit.

"Wait, Paul, poke your head in the door and ask Lizzie to bring out an extra glass of iced tea."

Paul didn't have to, because at the same moment Lizzie came through the door, carrying two full glasses and a plate with a sandwich for her *vader*. He accepted them, thanking her. She went back inside. Paul handed the plate and a glass to her father and then sat down, taking a long sip from the other glass. The tea had a touch of sweetness added to it. He settled into the chair. Next to him he heard Joseph's chair squeaking against the wooden floor.

"I can fix that noise with a little wood glue if you like."

"*Nee*. I like the sound. I find it comforting."

They sat in silence, both looking out over the railing at the front yard, where a few of Lizzie's Rhode Island red hens pecked their way around the yard. Their russet-colored feathers looked even richer in the late-afternoon sunlight. The sound of a hay mower mingled with the clucking of the hens. Paul knew Joseph Miller took great pride in his farm. It must be hard for him to let others do his work and upkeep.

"You need to stop abandoning your own work to come here, Paul."

"I'm not abandoning my work. I was only taking my turn helping out in the fields. It was no trouble at all."

"I was hoping you came by to see Lizzie."

Sitting next to each other in the rocking chairs brought Joseph eye level with him. The man used that vantage point to make his point. Looking him square in the eye, Lizzie's father's gaze hardened a bit.

"You and Lizzie have known each other your entire lives. If not for the accident, things might be different for the two of you right now. I know that the Lord has plans for all of us. But having my oldest daughter living in another community, leaving one of my children dead and one scarred…well, that's a plan I haven't been able to figure out."

It shocked him to hear this man speak about that day. Did Joseph truly know of the guilt that Paul carried with him? Still, his visits Lizzie were never about his guilt. They were friends, and right now she needed each and every one of her friends to help her and her family through this rough patch.

He knew he should set this man straight, but instead Paul said what came to mind first. "Mr. Miller… Joseph, it's not for us to question *Gott*'s motives."

"I'm left with little choice at the moment. This heart attack has left me with a lot of time to think. And I'm not one who likes to waste time doing that. I'd rather be out, working my land and tending to my cows. But this recovery has set me to thinking that I need to get my youngest daughter married off."

He'd known that this was where the conversation had been heading. After all, Amish men very rarely wasted time sitting about in the daylight hours. Still Paul found himself feeling uncomfortable at the idea of discussing marriage…particularly Lizzie's marriage.

"Without a son and with one married daughter living over an hour away in another district, I need to consider what's going to happen to my farm."

"I do understand, but I'm not a farmer. I'm a furniture maker."

"*Ja.* This I know. Perhaps I will find another man for her—one who likes to farm. Even considering her..." Struggling to find the words, he swallowed and then said, "Even considering her disfigurement, she would make a fine wife for any good Amish man."

In that very second something occurred to Paul; he'd never once considered Lizzie's scar as a disfigurement. He thought about her inner beauty and how she carried that over into her artwork. He wondered what Joseph would say if he knew of his daughter's talent? He heard some shuffling noise near the door. Turning his head, he looked past where Joseph sat. Narrowing his eyes, he tried to see through the shadows. Was there someone hiding behind the screen door? He couldn't tell.

Anger rolled through him, causing his shoulders to tense up as a knot formed in the pit of his stomach. Her life over the past decade had not been an easy one. Because of this he wanted Lizzie to be more than just someone's wife. She deserved to be loved and cared for. A surge of protectiveness welled up from inside of him. He clenched and unclenched his hands. Paul had been working hard to set up his own business; even if he wanted to do as Joseph suggested, he couldn't. Opening a new store always carried a risk of failure, and he wanted to be secure in his own right before he offered courtship to any woman.

The time wasn't right.

Looking at the man who so desperately wanted to keep his family and farm going, the only thing he could think to say was, "I'm sorry. I know this is a difficult time and you want to be sure Lizzie is safe."

"That isn't all I need. I need to have this farm carried into the next generation. Lizzie is the only hope I have left."

He nodded at Joseph. "I understand." Paul was only now beginning to understand the pressure Lizzie had been under. It was no wonder she'd turned to stealing time to work on her sketches.

Paul needed to find a way to give her some time to simply relax. Remembering the images he'd seen of the field she'd been working on, he thought maybe he could convince her to go there with him. He knew her art was a talent given to her by *Gott*. She should be able to use it freely. Maybe she'd be interested in a picnic. Out of the corner of his eye, he studied her *vader*, thinking how happy the man would be if Paul and Lizzie shared an afternoon together.

"Joseph, would it be okay with you if I took your daughter on a picnic?"

"That depends on what your intentions are."

"My intentions are to take your daughter on a picnic, as a friend."

Joseph leaned his back into the rocking chair, rubbing a hand down his gray beard. Paul could almost see the wheels turning inside the man's head. He knew Joseph wanted this to be the beginning of courtship.

"I suppose a picnic with you, as a friend, is better than nothing. You'll bring one of your *bruders* along." Turning his head toward the screen door, Joseph called out, "Elizabeth! Come out here, now!"

Lizzie practically flew through the screen door. "*Vader!* Are you all right?" Her face looked ashen with fear. Behind her, her *mamm*, who must have been thinking something was wrong, too, stood clutching the neckline of her dress.

"I'm fine." Turning to Paul, he waved a hand between them, demanding, "Ask her."

Left with little choice, Paul stood, walked toward Lizzie and asked, "Would you like to go on a picnic with me?"

Chapter Five

The midmorning light filled the far corner of Lizzie's bedroom. After finishing her morning chores, she'd come back in to be sure she had everything she needed before Paul came to pick her up. Even though it was a rare occurrence, other than on the Sabbath, for there to be a day off, Paul had managed to free up this particular Saturday afternoon. Walking around her bed, she went over to her dresser and gently slid the bottom drawer open. There, in a neat pile, lay all of the drawings she'd worked on over the last eight years. She took the top two pieces of drawing paper out and placed them next to her on the floor. Then she picked up the drawing pad, gathered the selected drawings and straightened up.

Lizzie took a canvas bag off the hook behind the bedroom door and put the artwork inside of it. She cast a glance toward the box on top of her nightstand, the place where she'd put the bag Paul had given her. She'd taken the paints out twice since the day he'd brought them over. She'd been surprised when she'd found three watercolor paintbrushes resting at the bottom of the bag. Lizzie had dabbled with the colors a few times. She was amazed at how the shades seemed to float across the paper. Seeing the colors bringing her work to life had made her heart soar.

Nibbling on her bottom lip, she waged a battle with temptation. Her parents would not be happy if they knew about this frivolous gift Paul had given her. Though Lizzie knew painting landscapes wasn't exactly forbidden, her *vader* would consider her art a waste of precious time. Today was supposed to be a day off for her. Surely she could use some of that time testing out some more of these paints. Finally she opened the lid on the box and took out the paints, tossing them into the canvas bag. Looping the straps over her shoulder, she walked out of the room.

Her *mamm* met her at the front door, holding a wicker picnic basket in her hands.

"Here, I fixed some extra food for you and Paul. There's water and soft drinks, along with a blanket. I think I remembered everything you put out last night."

"Danke," Lizzie said, taking the basket from her. She felt a strange fluttering in her stomach. It was as if there were something different about this day, something special. Even though Paul would be bringing one of his *bruders* along, Lizzie still felt like this could be more than just two friends going on a picnic. Smiling at her *mamm*, she stepped out onto the front porch.

Paul had just arrived. She spotted his younger *bruder* Abram sitting on the back of the buggy with his feet dangling over the edge.

He called out a hello and Lizzie waved back.

She waited on the top step while Paul stepped down from his family's buggy. He tipped his hat to her. She noticed he had on black pants and a white shirt. He'd even changed out his straw hat for his Sunday one. Lizzie thought Paul looked very handsome today.

"Good day, Lizzie." His glance slid to her *mamm* as he added, "Good day, Mrs. Miller."

"Good day to you, too, Paul. You've picked a fine one for a picnic."

"This day wasn't my doing—it's a gift from *Gott*." Paul beamed as he looked up at the crystal-clear blue sky.

"*Ja*. That it is," her *mamm* nodded in agreement. "I'm afraid Joseph is out for his morning walk. He'll be sorry to have missed you."

"I take it he's feeling better."

"So much better now that he's moving around more."

"That's good to hear." Paul swung his gaze back to Lizzie, saying, "Are you ready?"

"I am."

He took the basket from her as she climbed up into the buggy with the canvas bag. After she got settled, Paul went around to the other side and joined her, tucking her basket at their feet next to a smaller one. Lizzie suddenly felt like a bundle of nerves. She placed the bag on the seat between them. She fidgeted with her prayer *kapp*, then ran her hands along the front of her white apron, which covered her favorite pale blue skirt.

Paul glanced at the bag as he picked up the leather reins and urged the horse forward. "Are those your paint supplies?"

"*Ja*. I hope you don't mind that I brought them along."

"*Nee*. I'm anxious to see what you've accomplished since I gave them to you," he replied, concentrating on the roadway ahead.

"Not much, I'm afraid. I did take them out a few times to try them. I love the way the colors move on the paper. Some of them look like bright gems. But others..." She paused to grimace at her mistakes. "If you're not careful when you mix them, they come out looking like mud."

Beside her, Paul chuckled. "Sounds like using watercolors can be a bit of trial and error. You must have a lot of drawings stored away. I mean, since you've been doing this for some time now."

She nodded. She'd never taken the time to count how many drawings she'd done over the years. She only knew that the bottom dresser drawer was filled to the top. And that didn't take into account the box of drawings she'd stashed away under her bed. Over time her eye had become keener for spotting things that would be good subjects. Like her recent drawing of the barn.

Looking off in the distance, she spotted a small

herd of deer grazing near the edge of a tree line. Perhaps one of these days she would try her hand at sketching some animal figures.

"Still, today will be a fine day for picnicking *and* painting."

Out of the corner of her eye, Lizzie stole a glance at Paul. He seemed unusually interested in her artwork. The horse pulled the weight of the buggy along at a good clip. They rode by Sadie's house. Lizzie had seen her friend a few days ago and had decided not to mention her picnic with Paul. Sadie would have made a bigger deal out of this than it was. Today was nothing more than two friends spending an afternoon together. And yet Lizzie felt an energy coming from Paul that set her nerves on edge again.

Trying to alleviate some of her unease, she asked, "Where are we going to for this picnic?"

"A place I know you will love," Paul answered as he turned the horse to the left onto Angel Hill Road.

The mare trotted along the road that divided Miller's Crossing in half. Lizzie hadn't been out this way in a very long time. The horse began to slow as it climbed a steep incline. Lizzie felt bad for the animal and was glad when the land leveled out a bit. The wide vistas of Chautauqua County, New York, spread out before them. Rolling hills gave way to wooded areas. Off in the distance small lakes dotted the landscape.

"This is beautiful," she whispered, already imagining how this would look on paper. She would use greens and a touch of gold hues to bring out the early hint of fall color.

Lizzie's heart raced at the thought.

Beside her, Paul worked the reins with such confidence, Lizzie felt a bit in awe of his driving skills. The buggy slowed as it rolled down one steep hill, then crested up high on a rise where a beautiful church sat. The simple square structure had gray-colored siding and white trim surrounding it. A tall steeple rose from the center of the pitched roof. Two windows flanked the front door. A sign proclaimed this building to be the Clymer Hill Reformed Church.

Lizzie knew it to be a church used only by *Englischers*, and she realized how lucky those parishioners were to be able to worship here in the glory of God.

After parking the buggy in the shade of the building, Paul helped Lizzie down from the seat. Abram jumped down from the back and raced around to the front of the buggy. "I'll go find us a spot to sit," he called out, running away.

Lizzie laughed at his energy. She waited while Paul gathered the picnic baskets and her canvas bag. They walked side by side along the edge of the parking area, coming to where the pavement met the soft earth of a hayfield. Before them lay a vista powerful enough to take one's breath away. From up here they could see the farms and a patchwork of green-and-brown fields. Dust from a plow billowed up in the distance.

Paul extended his arm, pointing to their right, "That's your house, right over there."

"That little speck? Oh, my!"

In her excitement she gripped the side of his arm, her fingers flexing against a hard wall of muscle. "Wow! I wish I could come here more often. It's too far to walk, though. These steep hills are not easy on the legs. All these years I've been missing out."

With her gaze still on the horizon, Lizzie took in the beauty. Paul had discovered a lovely spot. She was glad he wanted to share this with her. Happiness welled up from inside of her. Lizzie let out a delighted laugh.

The sound of Lizzie's laughter was music to his ears.

"*Ja.* It would be a difficult walk. I only come up here in a buggy. It's a great spot to sit and think."

"Do you come here often?"

"I used to sneak up here when I was a young boy. And then after David's death… I came here a great deal." He'd watch the sky change colors in the evening light. He'd think about how horrible that day had been as he'd prayed for forgiveness. He still couldn't be sure if he'd been given that yet.

The beauty of this place was something to behold. Whoever the person was who'd picked this as a location for the church had done so knowing how these wonders could restore a person's faith. Even through all the pain and suffering that David's death had left behind, the one thing that had never wavered was his faith. The doubts he had were solely within himself.

"I can understand why you came here. There's a peace about this place. I think it's a wonderful spot to sit in reflection."

He looked down at her, taking in her honey-colored hair and her perfectly placed prayer *kapp*. He looked at her face, seeing a wistful smile appear and maybe hope reflected in her eyes.

Taking another chance, he spoke in soft tones, saying, "And I think it might be a wonderful place to paint."

With her gaze still fixed on the horizon, she nodded.

Paul wasted little time in joining Abram at the spot that he'd picked out for them on top of a rise. From here they could see out over the fields. Spreading the blanket out, he was anxious to see what Lizzie had brought in her bag. But first he had to deal with his *bruder*, who was running circles around them.

"Abram. You need to slow down," Paul gently warned him. "The last thing I need is for you to fall and get hurt."

"I'm not going to get hurt. Can I take my sandwich and go over there?" Abram asked Paul, pointing to a stone wall at the edge of the field.

"*Ja*. But stay where I can see you," Paul told him, handing Abram a bag with an egg salad sandwich.

Then he turned his attention back to Lizzie, watching as she took out a sketch pad, the paints and supplies. His breath caught when she pulled out two larger sheets of paper. The images were stunning.

Reaching across the blanket, he asked, "Might I take a closer look at these?"

"I'm afraid they're not very good."

"Lizzie, how can you say such a thing? These are beautiful." *Like you*, he almost added. But instead he turned his attention to the image of a field that he recognized.

As he continued to look at her art, she arranged her paints and brushes on the blanket. She asked him if there might be a plastic lid she could use in the picnic basket. Setting the artwork down, he opened the top of the wicker hamper her mother has sent and found a round container of macaroni salad. He took the lid off and handed it to her.

"Will this do?"

"Hand me that bottle of water, please." She pointed to one of two lying side by side next to the sandwiches.

He did. She unscrewed the cap and dumped a few drops of water on it, cleaning it off.

Paul wondered what she was going to do with the lid and water.

"I'm going to put the paints on this. And the water will help thin out the colors," she explained.

"Ah. I should have known."

"I went to the library last week and looked up some books on watercolor painting. It seems the author of this one book is a very famous watercolorist. That's what they're called, you know. I couldn't spend too much time there, as I was supposed to be picking up some items for *Mamm* at the general store. But I did have time to learn how to blend colors. That's what I've been working on."

While Lizzie worked in her sketch pad, Paul set up their lunch. Sandwiches, salad, drinks and chocolate whoopie pies for desserts. It appeared their *mamms* hadn't left a thing out of those baskets. He knew both sets of parents were hoping for a good outcome from today. He rolled his shoulders, preparing himself for the conversation. And he had something else he needed to discuss with her, an idea that could help her family.

But first things first. He was starving.

"Which sandwich do you want, egg salad or tuna salad?" he asked.

"Why don't we split them?"

"Good idea." He found paper plates and napkins at the bottom of the basket his *mamm* had packed. After carefully unwrapping the sandwiches, he arranged the halves on two plates.

After giving her one of the plates, he took the plunge. "You know, I've been talking with your *vader* about us."

She'd been working on the top of her painting. Her brush strokes of blue tones spreading across the paper. He realized it was the same color as the sky above them. She paused midstroke, looking up at him, seeming to ponder his words. Lizzie set the artwork aside and put the brush on the lid. Then she picked up the half of the tuna salad sandwich and started nibbling at the edges of the bread.

Clearing his throat, Paul made a great effort out of studying the egg salad sandwich he'd been holding. He took a healthy bite, and then in four more, the sandwich was gone. Beside him, Lizzie continued to nibble away at hers. Not saying a word.

In a fit of frustration, he said, "Don't you want to know what we've been discussing?"

Calmly she placed her half-eaten portion back onto the plate. She picked up the water bottle, twisted off the cap and took a sip. Then she set the bottle back in the exact spot where she'd picked it up.

She avoided looking at him. "A few weeks ago, I overheard the two of you talking about our courtship."

His heart sank. Had she heard everything? Her *vader*'s words had sounded harsh to Paul. He could only imagine how Lizzie had been affected. He took her hand in his, feeling her fingers tremble. Rubbing his thumb across her knuckles, he wondered at all she had endured. Lizzie deserved so much better. She deserved happiness. She deserved to do her artwork out in the open. The world needed to see her talent. But first he needed to talk about their relationship.

She beat him to the punch by saying, "Paul, I know a courtship between us would make our families happy. But..." She stopped, pulling her hand from his. She rubbed it along her scar. "My *vader*, he needs to be sure his farm will last into the next generation. We've talked about this before, you and I. You are not a farmer. Besides, this—" she indicated the side of her face "—is going to make it difficult for me to find a husband."

Shaking her head, she looked down at the painting she'd been working on. Lowering her voice, she added, "I'm just not ready for any kind of a relationship."

Anger surged through him, causing him to question the reasons for things he couldn't change. He wanted to fight for her. But most important he wanted her to fight for her own confidence. He wanted to see Lizzie happy and at peace. And he cared for her enough to know that if she couldn't see a way to make a life with him, then he prayed she would find happiness with someone else.

As he sat there looking at her, willing her to change her mind, Paul realized he didn't want Lizzie to have a life with anyone else.

"Lizzie. I don't believe this to be true. You are warm and caring. You love to cook. I think you need to give yourself time to think about a courtship."

"*Nee*. I will find another way to help my family."

By now he'd learned to recognize the stubborn set to her jaw and knew she was finished with that conversation. But Paul saw the opportunity to discuss his next idea and took it.

"There is a way for you to do just that."

She looked back at him. "What are you talking about?"

He shifted his weight on the blanket, leaned back and rested his weight on his elbows, stretching out his legs and then crossing them at the ankles. When he was sure he had her attention, Paul nodded in the direction of her watercolors.

Lizzie pursed her mouth into a tight line. She shook her head. "Paul Burkholder, I want you to get whatever thought you have about my art out of your head this instant."

"You haven't even heard me out. At least let me tell you my idea."

She folded her arms across her chest. Her eyelashes dipped, and he could see her waging a silent battle. Paul waited. And waited. And waited.

Just when he thought she would never respond, finally she said, "All right. Let's hear it."

Chapter Six

Pushing off his elbows, Paul sat up tall on the picnic blanket. "I want to sell your paintings at my store. They are stunning and I know that the *Englischers* would love them as much as I do. I can make all of the frames for them. And Lizzie, all the money you make from these could help your family."

"Nee!" Suddenly she stood up. With her hand on her hips and her back rigid, she stared him down.

Her eyes were filled with a sharp determination, but he also saw something else around the edges. Her expression softened. She stepped over the paintings she'd created, then walked off the blanket. Paul started to go after her. Lizzie wandered a few feet away from their picnic spot. He wanted to give her time to think about his offer, but there wasn't a lot of time to be had. Over the past couple of weeks, he'd been working day and night, getting his shop ready to open. He'd done what they call a soft opening this past Friday and it had gone quite well.

Paul walked up beside her, placing his hand on her shoulder. He had to convince her to do this. "Lizzie, I need you to think seriously about my offer. You need to trust me when I tell you this will work." Pausing to let his words sink in, he repeated, "Selling your paintings can help you and your family."

"You need to understand, no one knows I do this. No one except you, Paul. And I trusted you not to tell anyone."

Taking her by the shoulder, he spun her around to face him. "I haven't told a soul about your work."

He watched as she took in a deep breath and then exhaled. It hadn't been until after he'd come to help with the Millers' chores that the full extent of the their hardship had hit him. On the surface the farm looked like it was running well, but up close, Paul could see where the barns were run-down, in need of paint. And some of the equipment was in need of repair. This plan had to work. Lizzie selling her art could be the only way to help her family make ends meet. And like it or not, she was the only sibling left who could do anything to help her family. He had to make her see this.

She continued to shake her head. "I'm not like you. I'm not strong enough to go against my *vader*'s wishes."

Her words stung him. Did she think his decision hadn't been hard? "You are wrong about that. I thought long and hard before deciding on what would be best for myself and my family. You and I talked about this. You know how I felt."

"I didn't mean to insult you. I'm upset that my life can't be what everyone thinks it should be. But I don't want sympathy, either," she explained, stepping away from him.

Dropping his arms to his sides, he realized something Lizzie didn't see: she was far stronger than she or anyone in her family thought. He knew she could make this choice, but he didn't want to push her so hard that she would retreat back to the safety of her home. Paul knew she rarely left the farm. He knew how she planned her trips to the village on days that weren't busy ones. Just the other day he'd seen her waiting in the shadows outside of the general store, making sure the place was nearly empty before going inside.

He needed to tread lightly. So he tried a different tactic.

"Fair enough. How about this? We don't tell anyone who the artist is. The intrigue of your anonymity would certainly add a certain mystery to the work." He gave a shrug. "I think you might find that you do very well in my store."

She remained silent, though he knew she'd been listening to him. Paul turned, walking back to the blanket. He heard a gasp and looked over to make sure Lizzie was okay. But then he saw what had caused her reaction. Toward the horizon, where the earth met the sky, was a row of soft, billowy white clouds. Brilliant rays of golden sunlight streamed toward the earth, folding them in a warm glow.

Hope surged through him, filling him with *Gott*'s love and peace.

Lizzie faced him. "I'll think about what you've asked. Let me pray on this. Can you allow me that one thing?"

Feeling as if the weight of the issue had lightened a bit, Paul nodded. "Okay. But—"

She put her hand up. "No buts, Paul. You need to let me figure this out. My way."

"I can do that," he agreed, picking up the empty paper plates and packing them back in the picnic basket.

"Let me help with that," Lizzie said, coming over to join him.

She grabbed the water bottles and tossed them into the nearest recycling bin. Their hands collided when they both reached for the salad container. Paul felt her jolt of surprise, yet still he allowed his touch to linger on her hand for a few seconds longer than was proper. She tilted her head, looking into his eyes. A hint of a blush appeared high on her cheekbones. He captured her gaze with his. He saw her doubts and fears mingling with something else…hope.

"This is all going to work out." Lowering the tone of his voice, he whispered, "I promise, Lizzie."

She moved away from him, busying herself with putting her paints and watercolors away. "We need to be getting back."

"*Ja.* I don't want your parents to worry," he agreed, and then added, "Before you make up your mind, will you at least come by and visit Burkholder Amish Furniture Store?"

They worked together to fold the blanket. Then Lizzie took the blanket from him, saying, "*Ja*, I can do that."

There was a bit of morning drizzle the next day, followed by a severe thunderstorm. Lizzie stood at the only window in her bedroom, watching as the remnants of the dark clouds blew across the sky. The willow tree in the side yard bent in the wind, its light, feathery branches dancing along the rain-soaked earth. Tiny rivers of water flowed in front of the barn, trailing along the driveway. She knew the neighbors who still came by to help her *vader* on the farm were waiting out the storm. Since everyone would be getting a late start, she decided to take the extra time in prayer.

Kneeling beside her bed, she folded her hands and closed her eyes, and she said a silent prayer. "*Gott*, thank You for the rains to keep our crops growing. Thank You for watching over my *vader*. Give him the strength he needs to continue to heal. Bless my friends and family. Watch over my friend…" She paused, thinking of the hard choice Paul had made to take his furniture business into the village. She worried about this idea of marriage that both of the men had. Lizzie didn't know how to pray about that. Then she thought about the path Paul wanted her to take, with her artwork in his shop.

Lizzie so wanted to do the right thing. Framing

her thoughts, she continued with her prayers. "Please watch over my friend, Paul Burkholder, and guide him in the way You see fit. And please show me the path You want me to take. Amen."

Pushing her hands against the mattress, which was covered in a simple yellow bedspread, she rose, brushing her hands down the front of her dress. A sliver of sunlight spilled through the windows, bringing light into the room. The storm had finally passed. Going downstairs, she went into the kitchen and began to gather the ingredients for the loaves of bread that needed to be baked. Because of the two risings needed to get the loaves just right, the process would take most of the day. Lizzie planned on having the dough set for its first rise before the next round of workers arrived.

Before she knew it, a few hours had passed. She was in the middle of making honey butter when there came a light tapping on the front door. After grabbing a dampened towel from the edge of the sink, she wiped her hands on it as she made her way to the door. A smile popped onto her face when she saw not only her cousin, Rachel Miller, but her friend Sadie standing on the other side of the screen door.

"Come in! Come in!" Stepping aside, Lizzie beckoned them to enter. She saw right away that the women hadn't come empty-handed. Sadie carried in a wicker basket full of fresh vegetables, while Rachel brought in big clear jugs of what looked to be iced tea.

"I wasn't expecting anyone to stop by this soon.

I've just put today's bread loaves into pans for their last rising."

Lizzie looked at Rachel, who seemed to be beaming with joy. Her light blond hair was swept up in a bun, with her prayer *kapp* resting neatly on top of it. With her wedding only a few weeks away, she imagined Rachel must be getting excited.

She patted Rachel on the arm. Looking into her pretty hazel eyes, she said, "I'm so pleased you came by."

Sadie, in her usual spirited way, pushed past them, bustling into the kitchen. "We've come to lend you a hand. I imagine it isn't easy cooking for all those hungry men."

"There's only about half the crew we had the first week after my *vader*'s illness. He's starting to do simple chores again, *Gott* be praised," Lizzie told them as she took the basket of vegetables from Sadie and set them on the countertop near the sink. Then she took the iced tea from her cousin, thinking about her happiness at finding someone she loved to spend the rest of her life with.

"The day is drawing near for your wedding, *ja*? You must be getting excited."

"I am. Jacob and I are going on a train trip for part of our honeymoon." Rachel's eyes lit up with excitement. "It's going to be my first time on a train. But we just found out that my *aenti*, Rebecca, is unable to come to the wedding. She fell and broke her hip last week. She's the one I was most nervous about Jacob meeting. I know we're not supposed to have favorites, but she's my most beloved *aenti*."

Hearing the lilt in Rachel's voice and seeing the joy on her face gave Lizzie a pang in her chest. Her cousin had been most fortunate to marry for love. Arranged marriages were not all that uncommon within their communities. Arranged or not, Lizzie knew her chances of having a wedding of her own were slim to none. Not wanting to think about that anymore, she busied herself by preparing to get the loaves of bread into the oven.

She took off the damp cloth from the tops of the bread pans and set them aside. The air immediately filled with the pungent yeasty scent. Though she was tempted to poke a finger into the spongy dough, she knew better. In about an hour they would come out of the oven a delicious golden color, ready to be eaten. Behind her, Sadie and Rachel chattered away about weddings and the latest gossip. Lizzie had been so busy with her *daed* over the past weeks that she'd little idea what had been happening in their community outside their farm.

"And then I heard that Paul's brother, Abram, is considering *rumspringa*."

This declaration came from Sadie. "Did Paul mention this to you, Lizzie?"

Lizzie spun around, nearly toppling over a sheet pan that her *mamm* had left on the stove top. Reaching out, she managed to catch it before it fell.

"I haven't heard this." Slowly she turned to find

both women staring at her. "What? You both think that Paul and I have been gossiping together?"

"Maybe there have been other things going on, like the beginning of a courtship." Rachel wiggled her pale eyebrows at Lizzie. "He has been spending a lot of time here."

Lizzie's hands trembled, as she was reminded of Paul's conversation with her while they were on their picnic. She hadn't spoken to anyone about her feelings on the matter of a courtship, other than Paul.

She made a half-hearted attempt to shrug off Rachel's suggestion. "He's been putting in his fair share of time helping on the farm and he's been busy working on his new furniture shop in town."

Having been her closest friend since they were small children, Sadie noticed her discomfort first. Her brow furrowed in worry, she put her hand on Lizzie's forearm. Guiding her across the linoleum floor, she urged her to sit down in one of the wooden chairs that surrounded the plank table.

"*Es dutt mir leed.* I'm sorry if our chatter has upset you."

"Nee," she assured them, mustering up a tiny smile.

While Sadie gathered two more chairs to bring them into a little semicircle, Rachel took three glasses from the cupboard and filled them with the iced tea she'd brought. Lizzie took a deep breath, fighting the urge to break down and have a good cry.

"Look, Sadie, you of all people should know that there can never be anything more than friendship between Paul and myself. I can't be with him in any other way."

"I think you're wrong. This is a tight-knit community and no one would ever want to see you get hurt again."

Lizzie picked at her apron, and Sadie placed her hand on top of hers. "You need to think about getting married, Lizzie."

Tears sprang to her eyes as remnants of her recent conversations with Paul swirled through her head. "Who would want me? Who would want to wake up every morning and look at this?" Lizzie gave Sadie and Rachel a full view of the scarred side of her face.

"Lizzie!" Sadie's voice rose a notch. "No one cares about your scar."

"Listen to what Sadie is saying." Rachel tried to calm Lizzie with a soothing tone of voice.

"I am listening. And don't either of you dare give me the '*Gott* wouldn't give you more than you can handle' speech." The words came out in a choked whisper.

Sadie frowned as she said, "Lizzie, we're just trying to be helpful."

She hated the hurt she saw on their faces. Her stomach felt as if it were twisting into tight knots. Sadie and Rachel sat in patient silence, waiting on Lizzie. But she remained silent.

Finally Sadie spoke. Her soft, melodic voice quoted one of their community's favorite sayings. "Life is too short to stay mad for very long."

"I feel like I've been in limbo for a very long time," Lizzie admitted.

She'd been thinking about Paul's offer to her. He was giving her a way out; she only had to find the courage to take it.

"Maybe it's time to think about making some changes." Once Rachel and Sadie were situated, and they'd all taken a sip of their tea, she looked at her friends.

"Lizzie, we know it's been rough at your house. How is your *daed* doing?" Rachel asked.

"Much better, *danke* for asking."

Sadie leaned in a bit to scrutinize Lizzie. She shook a finger in front of her face. "*Nee, nee.* This is not about your *daed.* I know you've got the strength of an ox when it comes to this sort of thing. This sadness is about something else. Am I right?"

Lizzie blew out a soft breath, finally answering, "*Ja*, you are *recht.*"

"Rachel and I will keep your confidence. No matter what. You can trust us," Sadie added. Both of the women nodded at her.

Lizzie realized she wasn't ready to tell them about her artwork and Paul's shop yet. She needed time to think about everything. If the plan to sell the paintings didn't work out, then no one else would be the wiser. Still, Sadie and Rachel both sat forward on the edge of their seats, as if waiting for some big revelation.

"Paul and I went on a picnic."

"You and Paul went on a picnic!" Rachel let out a squeal as she clapped her hands together.

Sadie echoed her sentiment. "A picnic—you and Paul! Well, it's about time."

"It's not what either of you are thinking."

"Oh, yes, it is. *This* is the beginning of your courtship," Sadie quipped.

She wrung her hands together, feeling the tension set in her shoulders. "No." She shook her head with such vehemence that she nearly knocked her prayer *kapp* off.

"Then tell us what happened, Lizzie," Sadie said.

"Paul and I discussed the courtship idea everyone is so set on, and I told him the same thing I've been telling everyone else. It's not going to happen. We are good friends, that's all."

"I don't think that is all," Rachel chimed in.

Lizzie knew she could count on these women for anything, but on this subject, she would remain steadfast. There could be no future for her and Paul.

"I'm fine with our decisions. I'm fine with being an *alt maedel*."

"I'm so sorry," Rachel offered, shaking her head.

"Don't be sorry for me. You are going on an adventure with your new husband. I don't want you to worry about me." Lizzie's heart swelled with happiness for her cousin.

"While we're gone, I'm going to write to you every chance I get, and you will let me know how things are going with you and Paul."

"There will never be a 'me and Paul.'"

Silence descended on the trio of women. Lizzie bowed her head. Sadie continued to pat her hand. The clock on the living room wall struck three times at the same time the buzzer on the oven signaled the bread needed to be checked. Lizzie stood to shut the timer off and, using a pot holder, pulled the rack with the bread out of the oven. Normally seeing the golden color gave her such delight. But today not even the sight of the perfect freshly baked loaves could lighten her mood.

Behind her, Rachel said, "I have to be going. I promised Jacob I would stop off at his grandmother's house to pick up a wedding gift she has for us."

After Rachel left, Sadie and Lizzie stood alone in the room. Shrugging her shoulders, Lizzie said, "I need to keep my hands busy. I think I'm going to bake up some cream puffs as a special treat for the workers. Can you keep me company while I do that?"

"I'd like nothing better."

When she went to the pantry to take out the ingredients, she realized there wasn't enough baking soda for the dough.

"*Ach!* I've got to get better at making sure I stock up on my ingredients."

"I have to go into the village for a few things myself. We could walk together," Sadie suggested. "Besides, some fresh air might give you a different perspective on what we were talking about."

"I'm not so sure it will change anything. But a walk into town would be nice. Besides, I told Paul I'd stop by his new shop. Let me find my parents to let them know we'll be going. I think they are out in the garden."

She let Sadie go out the back door ahead of her. And after following the pathway around the side of the house, she found her parents outside, tending to the vegetables.

"Sadie and I have to go to the village. I need some baking soda. Do either of you need anything while I'm there?"

Her mother gave a quick shake of her head. "*Nee. Danke* for coming to ask."

"We shouldn't be too long."

She felt Sadie's hand brush along her arm. "We need to get going."

Saying their goodbyes, they headed off. At the end of the driveway, Sadie tugged on her arm, pulling her to a stop. "Now that we're alone, do you want to tell me what's *really* going on?"

Chapter Seven

Paul opened the door to the Burkholder Amish Furniture Store, stirring up a thin cloud of dust motes that danced along the sunbeam coming through the front window. He'd have to see to sweeping and dusting again. Already he'd found out that running a business took a lot of energy. But he had more than enough to spare when it came to seeing his dream come true.

Beneath his foot, the floorboards creaked as he walked into the large room. A long counter stood in the middle of the floor. The walls were covered with wallpaper that featured pink roses against a cream-colored background. A few years back this had been a ladies' clothing store. Three years ago the shop had closed when the owner had died and the family hadn't wanted to continue with the business. Until Paul had signed the lease papers, the single-story building had been vacant.

He set the take-out coffee he'd bought at Decker General Store on his way here, down on the windowsill just inside the front door. Putting his hands on his hips, Paul looked around, seeing all the work that still needed to be done. It wasn't difficult to imagine more of his furniture scattered about the room and the walls full of Lizzie's artwork hanging above his designs.

Paul took a small notepad and pen out of his vest pocket and began making a list of what still needed to be done. Though he'd been working around it, that ugly wallpaper needed to come down. Next up would be another thorough cleaning, and then seeing if the heavy counter could be moved over to one side of the room. He'd decided after the recent soft opening that the counter would work better if it was located off to the side.

Walking around the massive counter, he looked under the lip of the thickly planked top, checking to see if the structure was sound or if it was secured to the floor. It appeared that it was in good shape and was not attached to the floor. With a little brute strength, he felt sure that he and his *bruders* would be able to move it to another location. That would open up the space so he'd be able to showcase some of the larger pieces of furniture. He'd also been working on making simple wooden toys out of the scrap lumber from their shop. For some reason those items always grabbed the attention of shoppers. If he could get them in the door to look at those, chances were customers would be interested in seeing his handmade wooden tables, cabinets and chairs.

He continued to walk around, jotting down ideas as he went. He picked up his coffee and took a slow sip of the strongest black brew in the village. He took in the view from the window.

Across the street he saw a Plain woman walking with two children in tow. The stoplight in the center of Main Street turned red. A few cars and a blue pickup truck waited for the light to change. He saw two more Amish women walking into the general store next door. One of them turned and he realized it was Lizzie. He recognized her friend Sadie walking next to her. Paul started to wave to them, then realized they weren't looking in his direction.

He leaned against the edge of the doorway, thinking about his recent conversation with Lizzie. He knew that, for the moment, they both wanted different things, but in the end they wanted what was best for their families. Lizzie was so intent on doing right by her parents, he hoped she didn't lose sight of what she stood to gain. Paul still couldn't fathom the pain the Miller family had suffered over the years. He knew that he, himself, missed David every day. The loss had to be so much more for them. And Lizzie. He'd tried to be there as often as possible in the beginning, but over time they'd both grown older. Now he was entering his midtwenties, and his family was expecting him to settle down, choose a wife and have many children.

Of course he wanted all of those things, too. But he wanted them on his own terms. Well aware that if both *vaders* put their heads together, they could make a union between Paul and Lizzie happen, Paul still believed he should be the only one deciding his future. Most days Paul grappled with the fact that his father still didn't approve of his new business venture.

While Paul mulled things over, he waited for Lizzie to come out of the general store.

Fifteen minutes later the two women walked out of Becker's, and Paul didn't waste any time going out onto the stoop to beckon them over.

"Paul Burkholder! Look how you've transformed Davidson's Dress Shop! It's amazing!" Sadie said, bouncing up onto the steps, her excitement contagious.

"Come inside and I'll show you around." He tipped his hat to the women as they came to join him.

Lizzie cast a sidelong glance at Sadie, making him feel as if they'd been talking about him behind his back. Deep in his heart, he'd secretly hoped she'd come to town to tell him that she was going to take him up on his offer to sell her artwork in his shop. Paul offered a hand to help Lizzie up the steps. Shaking her head, she tucked a small bag into her apron pocket, freeing her hands. She put one hand on the old iron rail and stumbled on the step.

"Oh!" She let out a gasp as she clutched the rail to keep herself from falling.

Paul quickly caught her by the elbow. "Lizzie." He kept his voice low. "I've got you."

He looked at her pretty blue eyes and saw something he couldn't quite put his finger on. Trepidation? Wariness? Maybe a touch of excitement? He hoped she was bringing him good news.

Shaking off his touch, she said, "I'm fine. Now show us what you've got going on in here."

Stepping aside, he gave a slight bow and allowed both women to enter the shop ahead of him. Pride welled up inside him. This was the first time he'd shown this store to the people who mattered the most. He wondered if Lizzie and Sadie would think his idea as farfetched as his *vader* did. He found what he wanted more than Lizzie's consent to place her art on his walls was her agreement that he'd made the right choice.

"Welcome to the Burkholder Amish Furniture Store."

Lizzie tilted her head to look up at him. She opened her mouth as if to say something, then didn't. Her face softened as she spun about, taking in the store and all the furniture that was within. When she turned back to him, she tucked her lower lip between her teeth, pondering. He thought he saw just a tiny bit of approval reflected in her eyes.

"It's like I've been telling you—I've had this idea about bringing my furniture closer to the public for a very long time. And if the soft opening I had last week is any indication—" he paused to wipe his brow "—I think my shop is going to be quite successful."

Lizzie finally spoke, asking, "Your *vader*, he's finally come around to your way of thinking?"

"Not exactly." Paul walked over to the counter area.

Coming to stand next to the counter, she commented, "You're risking a lot going against him."

"*Ja*, but this feels right to me. It's like *Gott* has led

me to this." He saw the realization dawning on her face and knew then that Lizzie understood why he was doing this.

He needed to find his own way. Apart from his family. He was also doing this for his family, even if his father didn't quite see it that way. Like Lizzie made sure to take care of her parents, Paul was doing his best to take care of his, while at the same time finding a way to secure his own future. He'd prayed long and hard about it, looking to *Gott* for guidance, finally knowing this would be the right choice.

Pointing to the counter, he said, "I'm thinking this needs to be moved out of the way. The people who came in the other day had to walk around it in order to see the other stuff. I'd like to display some of the larger pieces in the middle of the room, with the chairs closer to the front. And I think putting baskets filled with wooden toys for *kinder* in the window might bring the customers in."

"I think you should put one of your chairs in the window. You make lovely chairs, Paul," he heard Lizzie say.

He gave her a quick smile. Her compliment meant a lot to him.

"Danke."

Sadie rubbed her hand along the smooth top of the counter. "Do you worry about your furniture being counterfeited? I've heard of this becoming more and more of a problem."

Well aware of this practice among *Englischers* to claim they were selling Amish furniture, he'd already found a way for someone to tell that they were getting an original Paul Burkholder piece. Paul had created a very small brand with the initials *PB* that he burned into the bottom of each piece of furniture he made. But he knew that little could be done to stop the counterfeiting. He wanted to focus on selling his pieces to customers who would appreciate owning a sturdy chair that would last for years. Right now he had no plans to sell his things anywhere but his own store.

"*Nee.* I have a mark that I put on all of my pieces."

Sadie nodded. "That's a very smart idea. Don't you agree, Lizzie?" Sadie cast her friend a look that Paul couldn't read. Something was amiss between the two of them.

Lizzie frowned.

Sadie gave an almost imperceptible nod of her head, her gaze swinging from Lizzie to him. Even though he had three sisters, Paul would be the last one to say he understood women.

He stuffed his hands into his pockets. It appeared the two of them were at some sort of a silent impasse. He worried that maybe Lizzie had come here to decline his offer.

"I think the rent for the place is affordable," he said to break the silence.

"*Ja.* That's *gut.* You don't want to get in over your head in the beginning. How much furniture do you have ready?"

She was obviously stalling. He could wait her out.

Paul answered her question. "I have a lot of the *kinder*'s toys, chairs—which seem to be quite popular—cabinets, some smaller end tables and three dining room sets." He nodded to the spot where he'd placed them in the middle of the store. "I put those on display and have already taken some orders."

"I like that idea." She looked around again, adding, "But this wallpaper has to go."

He chuckled. "What, you don't think the roses will look good next to my chairs?"

She wrinkled her nose. "Blooming on a bush, they would look lovely. On the walls of a furniture store, they are too frilly. You could take it down and then paint the walls a nice pale yellow. That would brighten the area. Maybe you could add some wicker baskets to the window display. The toys would look attractive stacked inside those."

"I'd like to add a big oval braided rug to the center of the room. One of the dining sets would go there. I can hang a few chairs up on the walls. Or I can save that space for your..." He stopped talking, realizing that he had no idea if Sadie knew about her friend's talent.

"You need to keep room for Lizzie's paintings," Sadie called out from the other side of the counter.

"I told her," Lizzie let him know.

Sadie gave them a mischievous smile. "I made her tell me." Strolling toward them, she added, "And if you want her to sell her paintings here, then my guess is she's very good at her art."

Paul blew out a relieved breath.

"I'm still not sure, Sadie."

"*Ja*. You are. What did we talk about on our walk all the way here, Lizzie?"

"You told me that what I do is no different than the Yoders' quilt making. That while their tapestry is cloth, mine is my watercolor on canvas."

"That's the truth. They make a decent amount of money selling their quilts to the *Englisch* tourists," Sadie said, coming up alongside her friend. "I could tell from the look on your face when you were discussing it with me just how happy your painting makes you. I haven't seen you so excited in a long time. Come on, Lizzie. Take Paul up on the offer."

She bowed her head, fingering the pocket on the front of her apron. Her voice quiet as she said, "There's still so much to work out."

He rested an elbow on the countertop, reminding himself that no matter how much he wanted this, he needed to tread carefully where Lizzie was concerned. He didn't want to scare her away, not when she was so close to finding a solution for her family. Not when she was so close to finding her own way.

"No, there's not," he commented. "You and I and, I'm assuming, Sadie—" he nodded in her direction "—are all in agreement that your work won't carry your name. No one outside of these walls will ever know who the artist is. I promise."

He cocked one eyebrow, looking directly at Lizzie. "So, are we in agreement?"

All of the time she'd spent in prayer, plus seeing Paul and Sadie standing there with hopeful expressions on their faces, made Lizzie finally realize that perhaps this was *Gott*'s answer. If they thought she had such talent, surely others might, too.

She looked at Paul, standing here in his shop, the Burkholder Amish Furniture Store. A feeling of pride welled up inside of her. To her, he was the bravest man she knew and not just because of this. Because he never backed down and he never turned away from her. Not once. She wanted so much for some of his bravery to rub off on her.

The thought brought a smile to her face. And before she knew it, she was agreeing to their partnership.

"Okay. I'll do it."

Sadie grabbed for Lizzie, hauling her into her arms and squeezing her so hard, some of the breath swooshed from her lungs.

"Sadie! Let me go." Laughter bubbled up from inside of her, as Sadie's excitement was contagious.

Sadie finally released her hold. Stepping back to look at Lizzie, she said, "I'm so happy for you. This is going to be *gut* for you and your *mamm* and *vader*. Just you wait and see."

"Let's hope you're right. I'm still worried what will happen if my *vader* finds out."

"He won't," Sadie assured her.

Lizzie was simply going to have to go on faith. After all, Sadie and Paul could be trusted. Since she planned on doing her artwork in private, she wouldn't be forced to deal with any of the customers. She could continue to keep to herself, and that suited her fine.

Turning around in a circle, she looked at all of the space, paying particular attention to the walls. It was difficult for her to imagine the paintings she'd done hanging there. Blinking, she found herself looking right at Paul. The corner of his mouth quirked up as he met her gaze.

Extending one hand, he offered, "Shall we shake on our deal?"

Chapter Eight

She nervously gave him a nod, then placed her hand inside of his. His large hand swallowed hers. She felt the rough callouses of his hard work etched along the pads of his fingers. Paul gently gripped her hand. In his hand she could feel his strength. When she looked into his dark eyes, Lizzie saw his deep and abiding affection for her. Lizzie knew he wanted more than just friendship, but she just couldn't give him what she didn't feel. Not right now. After a moment she pulled her hand out of his grasp. Putting her hand in the pocket of her apron, she found herself wanting to hold on to his warmth for as long as she could. But that was not proper for an unmarried Amish woman.

Sadie cleared her throat, reminding them both they were not alone in the room.

Paul rubbed his hand down his neck.

Lizzie fumbled with the bag in her pocket.

Sadie reminded her, "We should be getting back. We don't want to worry your parents."

Paul's gaze finally slid away from her. He picked up his notepad and pen, and then he walked them to the door. "I'm going back your way—why don't you let me give you a ride?"

"That would be nice," Sadie responded.

Snapping out of her thoughts, Lizzie added, "*Ja.* I need to get back to the house if I'm to get the cream puffs made up in time for supper."

"You're making cream puffs?"

She nodded.

"I don't think our neighbors realize how lucky they are to be helping out at your father's farm."

His compliment brought another smile to her face and a blush to her cheeks. She loved cooking and never saw it as an added chore. Lizzie did her best thinking while mixing and kneading dough of all sorts. And now she could spend some of that time thinking about her next watercolor project.

Closing the shop door behind them, Paul took a key out of his pocket and locked it. He brought the buggy from around the back of the building, and then helped Lizzie and Sadie up to their seats.

Even though Paul stayed off the main route that ran through Miller's Crossing, the traffic was heavy today. He kept the wagon partway on the shoulder of the road, giving the cars and trucks as much room as possible. Still, some of the cars whizzed by them, while others slowed to a crawl. A red SUV pulled to a stop in front of them. The passenger window rolled down, and a woman stuck her head out the window.

She pointed her cell phone at them and started taking pictures.

Both Sadie and Lizzie dropped their heads to their chins, averting their faces from the lens of the camera. Lizzie covered her face with both hands, wishing she were riding in her parents' buggy. At least then she'd have the sidewall to hide against. Paul turned his back to the right, doing his best to conceal her with his body. He gave the reins a gentle slap against the horse's hindquarter, urging the animal along as he ignored the tourist. The wagon jostled over a pothole. Lizzie's shoulder bumped against Paul's. She slid away from him so their bodies weren't touching. Eventually the car pulled away, but she knew it would be only a matter of time before another one came along.

Paul couldn't protect her forever.

Even though wintertime was not her favorite season, on summer days like this she longed for the quiet solitude that came with the snow-covered ground. The tourists stayed away from their community during the winter, and Lizzie did her best baking during those months. Not only did the house fill with wonderful scents, but the heat from the oven filled the kitchen with much-needed warmth. Now that she'd agreed to show her artwork at Paul's store, she could also use her time to do more watercolors. Her mind began to swirl with the images she'd like to put on paper. She wanted to continue to work on the one she started while she and Paul were on their picnic.

They went up and down one of the longer rolling hills. Lizzie lifted her face to the sky, feeling the warm breeze wash over her skin. A hawk circled above them. Down in the valley she could see fields of freshly mowed hay. The cuttings were in neat rows, waiting to be picked and formed into square bales by the baler. The road passed a fenced-in field where some cattle lazily grazed.

She cast Paul a sidelong glance, observing how deftly he handled the horse and buggy. The leather reins were looped loosely through his strong fingers. With a simple tug on those straps, he led the horse around a pothole. Today they'd made a big decision. She hoped with all her heart that it would be the right one.

"Do you think I was pressuring you?" His deep voice carried to her over the breeze.

She looked up at him in surprise, wondering how he'd known her thoughts. "*Nee*. I am doing this for all the right reasons. My only hope is that if my *vader* ever finds out where the extra money is coming from that he'll be able to forgive me."

"There won't be anything to forgive, Lizzie. You are only doing what needs to be done to save your family."

Lizzie wanted to believe him. But as they continued home, the self-doubts continued to swirl around her.

Beside her, Sadie fidgeted. *"Was iss letz?"* Lizzie asked. "What's wrong, Sadie?" When she continued to move around on the seat, Lizzie warned, "If you don't hold yourself steady, you'll end up dumping us both out on the road."

Leaning in close, Sadie whispered into her ear. "I'll tell you when we're alone."

She would just have to be satisfied with that answer. They rode in silence for the remainder of the trip home. Lizzie had Paul let them out at the end of the driveway.

Once they were standing alongside the buggy, Paul said, "Lizzie, I need you to bring me a half dozen of your watercolors. If you get them to me in the next few days, I can get them framed properly and hung on the walls."

Lizzie started to tell him that she'd changed her mind when he said, "You've got to trust me on this, Lizzie. All will be well. I'm sure of it."

Looking up at him sitting tall and oh so sure of himself on that buggy seat, it wasn't lost on her how handsome a man he was. Lizzie's heart skipped a beat. She didn't comment on what he'd said, only giving him a nod as they said their goodbyes.

Paul had barely pulled away before Sadie started talking to Lizzie. Her hands moved about, the motions punctuating each word. She was talking so fast that Lizzie could hardly keep up with what she was saying.

"There *is* something going on between you and Paul. And I think it's high time you both admitted it!"

She stared at her friend, frustration rolling through her. "We've had this conversation before. I told you we are just *gut* friends."

Sadie's eyes narrowed, and her mouth puckered. Folding her arms in front of her, she appeared to be taking a stance. For the life of her, Lizzie didn't know why Sadie had decided now was the time to discuss this matter.

"I've seen the way he looks at you, Lizzie. His eyes get this serious look in them. And you might not realize this, but you also get a look on your face."

"I do not!"

Sadie's head bobbed up and down. "*Ja.* You do."

Curious, Lizzie asked, "How do I look?"

"For one thing, you seem to blush *a lot* when you're with Paul."

Lizzie looked away from Sadie, embarrassed that she couldn't hide her feelings when she needed to the most.

Continuing with her assessment, Sadie added, "Plus think about all the things he's been doing for you that go above and beyond what all the other neighbors have done over the past few weeks." Lowering her voice, she said, "And Paul is selling your art to help your family because he cares a great deal for you. It's more than just friendship. And I'm thinking I might stand right here at the end of your driveway until you admit that what I'm saying is true."

Lizzie loved Sadie with all her heart, but right now she didn't want to discuss this. There was still so much that needed to be done before the day ended. She stepped around her friend. She started down the drive, but then she paused to look over her shoulder at her dear Sadie, who stood there trying to look formidable and failing miserably.

Lizzie gave her a lopsided smile, saying, "You can't stay there. Besides, it's time to start supper. Your *mamm* will be worried about you if you don't return soon. And I have to get my cream puffs made."

With that she hurried off, but not before she heard Sadie grumbling about how right she was and how wrong Lizzie was. She felt sorry she couldn't make her understand her feelings on this matter. Everyone knew that Paul Burkholder would make a fine husband. But not for Lizzie.

If he decided on a courtship with another woman, she would lose the special friendship she'd always had with him. A lump formed in the back of her throat. What would she do then?

As if to rid herself of this thought, she gave a quick shake of her head. She needed to concentrate on the here and now, and not think about what might lie in the future. Lizzie slowed her steps as she approached the front porch of her home. She heard the creak of the rocker. Pausing with one foot on the bottom step, she looked up to see her *vader* seated in his favorite spot.

"Lizzie. What kept you so long? Your *mamm* and I were beginning to worry about you." Her *vader* sat with his head resting against the back of the chair.

"I'm sorry for being late. After we were finished at the grocery store, Sadie and I ran into Paul. He gave us a tour of his new store."

"This store of Paul's, it is a big one?"

"He took over the space that used to be a dress

shop. The building is the one across the street from Decker's store."

"*Ja*. I know which one you're talking about." He sat up taller in the rocker. "I understand Paul's *vader* isn't pleased with his son's choice to open this store."

"Paul and his *vader* are working through this."

Her *vader* grunted his displeasure, saying, "Paul should abide by his *vader*'s wishes."

Shifting her weight from one foot to the other, she avoided his gaze, instead concentrating on the way the breeze carried the sweet scent of honeysuckle through the air. Knowing better than to say anything further on the subject, Lizzie asked, "Is *Mamm* inside?"

"*Ja*. She's working in the kitchen. Lizzie, would you do me a favor and bring me out my Bible?"

She pushed open the screen door, seeing her mother standing at the sink with a teakettle in one hand. She was looking out the window, her mouth tilted with a smile. Even on those hard days, her *mamm* always seemed to find something to smile about. She wondered what the cause of it was today.

"I've been watching the wrens working on their nests out in the birdhouses." She glanced at Lizzie and then, looking back out the window, quoted, "'By them shall the fowls of the heaven have their habitation, which sing among the branches.' Psalms 104:12. Come join me for a minute at the window."

"I have to fetch *vader*'s Bible."

"Do that and then come back."

Lizzie found the Bible on the stand next to her

vader's favorite living room chair. She grabbed it, took it out to him and then rejoined her *mamm* at the sink. Standing shoulder to shoulder with her, she saw the tiny lines surrounding her eyes and noticed the gray streaks running through her hair.

"Look at that one!" Her *mamm* let out a laugh. "The little bird has been pecking and poking at the others the whole time I've been watching them."

Lizzie saw the bird dip down and seemingly shove the other bird off the ledge of the birdhouse. The white house had three stories to it and was attached to a high pole, so it stood well off the ground. The birds worked at a frantic pace, emptying the space of the old nest. Soon a new one would replace it. Then the birds would move in, the mother bird would lay her eggs and in a few months' time a new family would hatch. The tiny fledglings would then take flight, leaving the nest forever.

She couldn't imagine ever leaving her family behind.

Her *mamm* turned to her and smiled. "Have you been having a *gut* day so far?"

"Ja."

"I heard from your sister Mary today. She and Aaron will be here in time for Rachel's wedding. She wanted to come sooner to visit, but two trips would be too much for them to make."

"They must be busy."

"*Ja*, Aaron is helping his family begin their harvest. It would be selfish to insist they come here now to visit your *vader* and then again for Rachel's wedding."

"I understand," Lizzie said, taking the baking powder out of her pocket. "I was going to make cream puffs for the workers, but I fear the day has gotten too late to start another baking project."

"You did all those loaves of bread. They'll be happy with that, for sure and certain."

Lizzie went to the counter, where she'd left out the ingredients earlier, and put them back on their shelves in the pantry. Then she and her *mamm* began to make the evening meal. From the porch came the sound of the rocker creaking. She heard the soft turn of a Bible page, then the muffled sound of her *vader*'s voice in prayer.

"*Gott*, I ask you for patience. Patience with my recovery from this illness that has taken over my body, patience for the harvest and patience for my daughter Elizabeth. Help her to see your way and the way that is best for this family. Amen."

Her *mamm* must have heard his words, too, because she turned to face Lizzie. She let out a long sigh.

"Do you remember the nerves that Mary had right before her wedding?"

Lizzie nodded.

"But then she discovered how much she loved Aaron and how good her life with him could be. Lizzie, your *daed*, he only wants what's best for you."

"His prayer said it all, *Mamm*. He wants what's best for his family. I'm not sure he cares what my feelings on the matter of marriage are. I know that I'm supposed to follow his wishes, but..." She let out a frustrated sigh, thinking about how, with Paul's urging, she'd committed to doing something to help her family. She just couldn't discuss this with them yet.

Absently she ran her fingertips over her scar. Thinking how her *mamm* had been the one to nurse her back to health. She'd been the one to sing softly to her at night as she had cried herself to sleep. Her *mamm* had been the one to clean her wounds, the one to hold her close and whisper comforting prayers. She'd understood Lizzie's anguish then, just as she understood Lizzie's uncertainty now. She realized now that she wanted to unburden herself. And she would have done so, but Lizzie knew it wasn't right to expect her *mamm* to keep her plan from the rest of the family. Especially her *vader.*

Lizzie vowed right then that if this venture became a financial success, she would tell them about it. But until that time, she knew it was better not to get anyone's hopes up.

Dropping her hands to her side, Lizzie said, "I have nothing to offer a *mann*."

Her mother reached out to her, tapping a finger lightly against Lizzie's chest, over the spot where her heart lay.

"You have everything a good *mann* would want, right here inside of you."

Perhaps it was the excitement of the day catching up with her, but suddenly Lizzie found herself wiping away tears. Taking her *mamm*'s hand in hers, she gave it a gentle squeeze, whispering, *"Danke."*

As they turned their attention to preparing and serving the evening meal, the day wound down and Lizzie was finally able to make an escape to her bedroom. Once there she shut the door and leaned her back against it, relishing the silence. Reaching down, she unlaced her black leather shoes, setting the pair right in front of her nightstand like she did every night. Then she slid off her dark stockings, enjoying the feel of the coolness of the evening air on her bare legs, and draped them across the bottom of her bed.

Padding across the bare floor, she made her way to the dresser, knelt down and opened the bottom drawer. She pulled out the first five drawings and spread them around her, trying to decide if any of them were worthy to sell. She twisted her mouth, trying not to grimace at how bad these looked. After pushing them aside, she hauled out the entire drawer and placed it onto the floor. Swishing her hand through the mess of paper, she gazed at the array of colors and sketches. Why did this choice have to be so hard? she wondered.

Finally she settled on six of her more recent works of the fields surrounding the Miller farm. The images were in various stages of the seasons. Her particular favorite was one of the field behind the barn. She remembered working on this during the early spring. The newly formed buds on the trees and the fresh green grass poking through the earth so recently ravaged by the winter's cold had captured her attention.

Looking at this watercolor, she found her spirit being filled with hope and warmth.

The remaining watercolors depicted the field transforming from spring to summer, eventually ending with a winter scene. Lizzie remembered how hard this one had been to work on. She'd only used a few colors from her palette. Adding grays and deep blues to the white paper, creating a very chilly looking winter scene. She hoped Paul's handiwork with the framing would add a touch of warmth to the starkness of this image.

Gathering the watercolors, she stood up and walked back to the bed, where she laid them out. She took the canvas bag she'd taken on the picnic off the coat rack on the wall and then very carefully, so as not to wrinkle the paper, slid them one by one into the bag. A tingling feeling of excitement wound its way along her spine. Lizzie had no idea what kind of money she could get for these, but she knew even the tiniest bit could help. The sale of her eggs, baked and canned goods at her roadside stand did help, but this, well, this could be far greater than anything she could imagine. She could help her family by taking some of the financial burden off them. Maybe her *vader* would eventually understand that Lizzie didn't need to take a husband in order to help run the farm the farm.

"Ach!" She was getting ahead of herself. Bowing her head, she asked the Lord once again for guidance.

"Dear *Gott*, thank You for giving me this talent. Help me to use it for good. Remind me that wealth in this world that has nothing to do with money. Thank You for looking over my family. Amen."

She raised her eyes to see the muted glow of the last of the setting sun reflected on the wall. She walked to the window and pulled aside the curtain so she could take in the full view of the final vestiges of the day fading to dusk. Her mind raced to memorize what lay before her. The colors in the sky meeting the horizon, melding together in beautiful reds and pinks. The barn in the foreground and the fencing surrounding the pasture all bathed in this stunning, soft, heavenly light. She heard the soft mooing of one of the cows and the rustle of hooves as the herd wandered over the pathway leading to the edge of the pasture.

She knew then that she was using her talent in the way that *Gott* had intended. If only she felt confident that her parents would be as happy about her artistic talents as Paul was. Pushing those thoughts aside, Lizzie hurried to get her sketch pad. Once she had it in her hands, she raced back to the window, where she spent the next hour sketching the glory as dusk became twilight. The more she sketched, the deeper her inner peace became. Gone were her self-doubts, and in its place came the knowledge that she could create beautiful images that captured the farm life that she'd grown up with.

The clock in the living room struck nine times. Lizzie looked up from the paper, surprised that so much time had passed. She started to flip the top of the sketch pad closed when her eyes caught sight of the barn and then the watercolor she'd started working on when she'd been with Paul. These two works had been giving her fits and starts since she'd first drawn them. The barn painting carried with it a lot of memories and pain, while the other reminded her of things she might never have in her life. Maybe one day soon she'd find the time to get back to finishing them.

Putting her supplies away, she got ready for bed. There was another busy day ahead tomorrow. But long after she'd made herself comfortable under the blanket, her mind was still wandering, full of thoughts of the future. She knew one thing for sure and certain. Tomorrow she would go to Paul's shop and leave him the watercolors she'd selected. No matter her doubts, Lizzie knew this was the only way she could help her family.

Chapter Nine

Paul stood inside the Burkholder Amish Furniture Store, watching the rain dripping from the awning hanging over the front window onto the sidewalk outside. What a dreary day, he thought, but a good day to putter around his shop. He'd finished making the small rocking chairs here and the larger pieces of furniture he was still making back at his *vader*'s shop. His *bruders* had come by late Friday to help him move the large wooden counter from the center of the room over to the side. He'd decided to use it as the cashier area. Not anticipating a lot of store traffic today, he'd decided to organize that space, in addition to rearranging the furniture displays.

He'd been reading up on what attracted buyers. Even though, he suspected, most of them came inside simply because they saw the word *Amish* on the store sign, Paul wanted to continue to keep things fresh inside the store. Looking around, he felt such pride in all that he'd accomplished in the short time he'd been open. He turned his attention to the stack of mail next to the cash register and was thumbing through it when a car pulled up in front of the store.

Recognizing the sedan, he went to the front door. He saw Helen Myers sitting behind the wheel of the car, and next to her in the passenger seat sat Lizzie. Helen leaned across the seat as Lizzie got out, giving him a big wave.

"Hey, Paul. Congratulations on your new store. I'll stop by when I'm not busy running errands."

Ducking under the overhang, he called out, "*Danke*, Helen."

Lizzie pushed the door closed and hurried to join him. The rain had turned to a spotty drizzle. He noticed the drops on her gray raincoat and in her honey-colored hair. She looked up at him and gave him a nervous smile.

"I hope you're not busy," she said in a soft voice.

He let out a laugh. "No! This rain is keeping everyone at home." Paul stood there looking at her, so happy she'd come by today.

"Can I come inside?"

"Oh. Yeah. Sorry about that. Here, let me get the door for you." It was then that he noticed she was hugging a canvas bag. When she entered the store ahead of him, he asked, "Are you in town to do some shopping?"

"*Nee*. I came to bring you these."

Before she even made it to the counter to set her bag down, Paul was hoping she'd finally brought him some of her watercolors.

"I was going to come yesterday, but we were so busy at the farm and my *vader* was feeling strong enough to do light work. So *Mamm* needed me to keep an eye on him." She let out a laugh. "He thinks he can do what the rest of the men do, but he's not ready for a full day just yet."

She set the bag up on the counter. Patting the dampened fabric, she turned to look at him. He could see the uncertainty clouding her eyes.

"Lizzie, this is very exciting!"

"Now, don't be getting ahead of yourself. I'm not even sure you'll like the ones I've chosen."

Stepping close to her, he caught the faint scent of lemons and noticed the tiny freckles on her nose. Softening his voice, he replied, "I know I'll love whatever you decide on."

"So, now you're going to be my number-one fan?" she teased.

"*Ja.* And I can guarantee I can sell whatever you bring here."

She dipped her eyelids and nibbled her lower lip, her hand still resting on the top of the canvas bag. He could see the edge of the watercolors peeking out. Paul knew it had cost her a lot to come here. He'd been so busy these last few days that he hadn't even seen her. But Lizzie had never been far from his thoughts. And now here she was, putting her talent and her courage on the line. He knew enough to handle the situation with great care. Lizzie could be as stubborn as the day was long. But this was a matter of trust, and the last thing he wanted was to frighten her away and send her running back home.

She reached into the bag to slide out the sheaf of papers. Paul raised his eyebrows. He shook his head in disbelief. Where had she been hiding these? he wondered. He'd only seen a few of the pieces she'd been working on. But one look at these images and he immediately recognized the hard corner of the barn, the white clapboard fencing, and the rolling green pastures dotted with new spring grass to be the field outside the barn where the Miller cows grazed. He helped her lay the artwork out on the counter.

"Lizzie. You've outdone yourself. These are lovely." Paul gazed from the artwork to her.

There was a sparkle in her blue eyes he'd never seen before. A light pinkish blush rose on her cheekbones. Her face took on a glow at his praise.

"I thought I could part with these the easiest. And I think they are what you're looking to put in your shop."

He ran his fingertips over the papers, nodding. "These landscapes will most certainly complement my work. Wow! Lizzie, I had no idea you had these."

"Oh, there are a lot more where these came from. But I must admit that my earlier work is pretty primitive. Art is like so many things in life—you need to keep practicing until you get it right."

Gathering her hand in his, Paul gave it a gentle squeeze. "You're right," he said, wanting to tease her, but instead his voice came out in a strained whisper.

She started to tug her hand out of his reach, but he

held fast. Lizzie held his gaze and he could see the struggle brewing inside of her. A bit of the sparkle left her. Her mouth tightened into a thin line. Paul didn't know how else to convince her that this was the *right* thing—that *they* could be right together. Somehow his thoughts were no longer just about Lizzie selling her art here.

Finally she said, "*Nee*, I'm far from right. Just think about what we're doing here today. I went behind my family's back. Even if the end justifies the means, I wish I didn't feel so bad about it."

He gave her a quick wink. "You want to know something?"

She cocked her head to one side, waiting for him to answer his own question.

"I'd be very worried about you if you didn't feel that way about coming here. Family is important to both of us. After all, they are the reason we are both here. Come on—I'm going to show you where all the framing will be done. We can take these to the back room and pick out the ones you think will be the best fit."

"How difficult can that be?" Lizzie asked.

He let out a laugh, thinking Lizzie had a lot to learn about the different types of wood that could go into making a frame. The right choice made all the difference.

Picking up the watercolors, he directed her to the back room. "I'll get you started."

As they entered the work area, he said, "You can

hang your coat on the hook over there." He pointed to a spot on the wall near the back door.

Once she'd done that, Paul showed her to the place where he'd set up the framing area. Corners of frames hung on a pegboard behind the counter. "You can pick out anything you want. I have the wood set aside for your frames."

Lizzie studied the choices. "I like the darker colors for the fall picture."

"That's a good choice." He took the corner piece from the pegboard and lined it up along the edge of the paper. *"Ja."* He agreed after seeing the match.

They couldn't have been there for more than ten minutes when Paul heard the front door open. "I've got to go see who came in. You keep working on this." He excused himself.

Walking through the doorway, back out into the front of the shop, Paul saw an Amish man bent over, looking down at one of the small children's rocking chairs he'd created last week. As the man stood and turned around, Paul recognized him. Squaring his shoulders, he walked across the floor to greet him.

"*Vader.* What brings you into the village on this rainy day?"

The man scrunched up his eyes, narrowing his gaze to look at his son. "I've come to see for myself this folly my son has entered into."

Paul called on every bit of strength and patience he had. His *vader* had no business coming here and insulting him. But his *vader* deserved his respect, no matter how hard it was to give at the moment.

"I don't see this as a folly. This is where my future lies."

The man scoffed. "That remains to be seen." Waving a hand around, he continued, "You've been working on some new pieces, I see."

"*Ja*, I have." Paul wondered if this meant he might be softening toward the idea of this store.

"I've a lot of work orders that need filling."

Since Paul had been talking with his *bruders*, he knew that wasn't exactly the truth. Their cabinet shop had been slow these past few weeks. Right before Paul had opened, he'd been working on finishing up the one big order they'd had all summer. All the more reason for his *vader* to realize that having a place here in the village was needed.

Shoving his hands in his pockets, he studied the man standing before him. Age was slowly making its way over his face, leaving behind wrinkles that fanned out around the corners of his dark eyes. His hair and beard were almost all gray. And now Paul noticed a slight hunch to his *vader*'s shoulders. He knew his vader was getting on in years, but he also knew the man's life as a cabinetmaker was nowhere near over.

"Paul, I'm going to get right to the point of my visit. I want you to close up this shop and come back to our business. I can't have you splitting us up."

"I don't think I'm doing that."

"*Ja*. You are. I know that Ben and Abram have been helping you here. Taking time away from their projects at the cabinet shop."

"They offered to come over after their day was completed. And you know I would never pull them from you," Paul said, feeling the anger and frustration at his *vader*'s narrow-mindedness creeping over him.

Aware that Lizzie could overhear what was being said, he tried again. "I want to do this. And I'm doing this for all the right reasons."

"What? You think coming here to be closer to the *Englischers* is our way? We need to stick together to keep our community growing. And here you are wandering off like you're having a *rumspringa*!" His *vader*'s voice rose.

Paul shook his head. Keeping his voice low, he said, "It's nothing like that, and you know it. I've told you again and again that I'm doing this to not only secure my future but to secure a future for the entire family."

His *vader*'s face reddened. "And what of *your* future? Have you plans for a courtship yet?"

Paul looked over his shoulder, trying to figure out how much of this Lizzie was overhearing. He didn't want to be having this exchange with the man. His *vader* came closer to him. Paul stood his ground.

"You know how to respect your elders."

"I do respect you."

Vader shook his head. "At the moment I'm not sure."

"Give me time to make this work."

"And what of your courtship?" *Vader*'s expression softened a bit as some of the anger left him.

Paul looked over his shoulder once more. Lizzie

was being awfully quiet back there. He wanted to answer the question, but he didn't want her to overhear his response.

"Paul, answer my question."

He frowned, replying, "I'm working on that, too."

"Listen to me, *sohn*. I know your life has had its share of ups and downs. And the Miller boy's death has stayed with you a long time."

Paul raised his eyebrows in surprise. He'd never discussed David with his *vader*. He wasn't sure how to respond, so he waited for him to finish his thought.

"You've always had a soft spot in your heart for Joseph's youngest daughter. Perhaps we should consider speaking to him..."

Holding up his hand, Paul interrupted his *vader*, stopping him from going any further. "*Nee*. Now is not the time to discuss that."

His *vader* sighed in exasperation. Some of the earlier anger seemed to have returned, because his voice rose again as he spoke. "I'm telling you, Paul, time is not going to stand still while you make up your mind about your future! If I need to intercede on both of these matters on your behalf, I will."

"Please, *Vader*, like I said before, give me time."

"You don't have long."

He escorted him to the door. Holding it open, Paul waited while he stepped out into the overcast day. The rain had stopped and the clouds were breaking up. Tiny patches of blue sky poked through the darkness of the sky. The lighter sky did little to clear the darkness from Paul's day. He waited as his *vader* got into the buggy and drove away. Turning, he went back inside to find Lizzie standing at the counter.

As he approached her, he attempted a smile, but failed miserably. "I'm guessing you overheard all of that?"

"*Ja*, I did," Lizzie answered.

She'd heard every word and her heart was breaking for him. Lizzie leaned toward him. She could see the confusion reflected in his eyes. She wanted more than ever to take some of that pain away, but she didn't know how. She put her hand on his arm. She felt his strong pulse thrumming under the pads of her fingertips. She felt the strength in the hard sinew of his forearm. Lizzie's heart melted just a bit. She didn't quite know what to do with this new feeling. She only knew that she wanted this sensation, whatever it was, to last.

For as long as she could remember, Paul had been there for her. And like his *vader* had stated, he'd been there as a constant friend and shoulder to lean on since the day David had died. She and Paul never really spoke about that day. Now she found herself wondering how he'd managed to cope over the years. She knew he'd a great faith in *Gott*, just as she did. Perhaps he drew his strength from Him. Maybe one day soon they would be able to speak about David and what a great loss his death had been for both of them.

For Lizzie's family it had also meant the end of the future for the farm. Without David there was no son left to carry on. She'd heard Mr. Burkholder telling

Paul he wanted to go to her *vader* to perhaps discuss a courtship. She and Paul had already discussed the reasons why that would never work. Paul was never going to become a farmer. He was a woodworker, a furniture maker. It was his life's calling. And her family couldn't afford to hire farm help. The only way to help her family continue to make ends meet was for her to sell her artwork. As she tried to hold fast to those arguments, Lizzie could no longer deny her growing feelings for Paul. But for right now, she wanted to make him feel better about today. About his encounter with his *vader*.

Squeezing the top of his wrist with her fingers, she said, "I'm sorry about the things your *vader* said to you."

"*Danke.* I wish he'd listen to what I'm saying. Truly listen. Doesn't he know that the last thing I would ever want is to make trouble for our family?"

"I'm sure he knows. But the old ways are hard to let go of, Paul." She took her hand away from his arm.

He frowned, creating lines on his forehead. She could almost see his mind racing with thoughts. This had to be so hard for him. But Lizzie could tell his talents lay here, in the beautiful furniture he made. She turned to look around the store. Her gaze found the twin set of children's rocking chairs. They were so adorable and would make a fine addition to someone's home. She pictured a small child rocking away, perhaps with a book or doll in their tiny hands. The thought gave her pause. She'd never thought about having children of her own and now here she was, standing next to Paul, looking at his creations and thinking such thoughts.

"Lizzie?"

The sound of Paul's voice interrupted her daydream. "Hmm?"

"What's got you smiling?"

"I..." She hesitated, blinking as her thoughts collided with the present. "I was just admiring your furniture. You do such fine work, Paul. You should be proud."

"I am. Now, if only my *vader* felt the same way you do."

"He'll come around."

"We are two peas in pod, you and I." His gaze softened as he looked down at her.

Lizzie's breath caught in her throat. She wasn't sure how to respond to his comment; instead she asked, "I decided on the frames. Would you like to come see what I've picked out?"

"Of course," Paul answered as he let her go ahead of him to the back room.

Lizzie couldn't contain her excitement. She wanted him to be as pleased as she was with her selections.

"Look at this barn wood." She had the sample piece of wood covering about half an inch of the painting. The weatherworn wood held a subtle gray patina. "I think I want that for all the frames. The look is fitting with the fields and that portion of the barn that's showing on the side."

He nodded. "I agree. This choice is much better than the darker frame you first looked at."

She set the artwork down, clapping her hands together. Lizzie couldn't remember the last time she'd felt this happy. She wanted to hold tight to the sensation. Paul must have felt her excitement, because he put his hand on her shoulder.

"I'm glad you're coming around to this idea."

"Me, too. *Danke* for pushing me to do this."

With a gentle nudge, he turned her to face him. "I'm so proud of you, Lizzie."

The look she saw in his eyes held more than pride. Lizzie's heart began to race as her stomach did the strangest little flip-flop.

She whispered his name. "Paul."

He gazed deep into her eyes, and she knew his feelings for her were more than just friendship. Lizzie pulled away from him. Even though she felt the shift in their relationship, she couldn't help thinking she wasn't ready for this.

Then Paul spoke so softly that Lizzie had to lean in to hear him. "One day soon, Lizzie Miller, you will know that you can trust what is going on between us with your whole heart."

Then Paul turned his attention back to the frame. Running his hand over the wood, he told her, "I'll get these made up tonight."

"All right." Gathering the canvas bag, she realized that she needed to be hurrying back home. "I have to go." She was almost to the door when she turned around and said to him, "I'm working on Rachel's wedding gift. Would you be able to make me up a small recipe box?"

"Of course. Are you going to be giving away all your special recipes?" he asked, grinning at her.

She laughed at him. "Not all of them. Just a few of my jam recipes."

"I'm sure Rachel and Jacob will love your gift," he added.

"I hope so." Lizzie paused in the doorway. She looked up at Paul as her stomach gave her that little flip-flop sensation again. She didn't like feeling confused about Paul. Gripping the straps on the canvas bag, she said, "I'll see you in a few days."

He gave her a nod and gently closed the door behind her.

Chapter Ten

The next few days flew by as Lizzie found herself rushing to complete her wedding gift. She'd already made up the blueberry and the blackberry jams. Today she planned on finishing up with a batch of apple butter. She loved making this recipe because it was a perfect way to use up extra apples. However, for her cousin's wedding present, she'd used only the finest Cortland apples. The entire kitchen smelled like warm apples and cinnamon. As she took the canning jars out of the hot water bath, she couldn't help but ponder her last meeting with Paul.

Lizzie had felt that their relationship was changing. For a long time now, she'd known his feelings were more than that of just a friend. Once again her long-held insecurities reared their ugly heads. She was having trouble imagining herself as a wife. As far as she was concerned, Paul deserved someone far better than her. And yet he stuck by her through the good and bad days. In her heart of hearts, she knew there weren't many men like him.

And in her heart of hearts, she also knew she no longer saw him as just a friend.

She picked up the stainless steel ladle and began scooping the apple butter into the sterilized canning jars. The warm, spicy steam wafted up out of the jar. She filled a half-dozen jars. Then she screwed the metal lids in place. When that was done, she lined them up alongside the other filled jars, admiring her handiwork. After the jams and butter were cooled, she planned on packing them up in a basket. Lizzie also had the recipe cards in a neat pile on the counter, waiting for the recipe box Paul had said he would make for her.

These three recipes were the ones that were the most popular at her roadside shed. She let out a contented sigh. These were the best choice for the gift.

She heard boots stomping on the porch and knew her *vader* had come up for his morning tea. Anticipating this, she'd set a teakettle over low heat half an hour ago. Taking it from the stove top, she set about making his favorite cup of tea. Simple black tea with two teaspoons of sugar and a dollop of cream.

"Hello, *Daed*," she called out as he came into the *haus*.

"*Dochder*. I see you've got my tea brewing. *Danke*." Sitting down at his usual spot at the table, he said, "I'll have you know it's a fine late summer's day out there. The last cutting is going to be this week. Just in time for your cousin Rachel's wedding."

Lizzie was looking forward to Rachel and Jacob's big day. Her sister, Mary, and her husband would be arriving soon. Her *mamm* had been cleaning out the spare bedroom all week. This very minute the freshly laundered sheets were hanging to dry out on the clothesline, flapping in the breeze.

"You look to be having a great day, *Daed*."

"I am at that, Lizzie. This morning I woke up before the light of dawn and for the first time did not feel the effects of my illness. The doctors were right. Three months later, I'm as fit as a fiddle again."

After setting the pitcher of milk in the refrigerator, Lizzie took him his tea.

"I think your sister will be here today."

Lizzie raised an eyebrow, curious as to how he would know that.

"I can't keep the surprise from you, not on a day as fine as this. Her letter last week let us know when she was arriving. That's why your *mamm* has been so busy getting that room ready."

It had been almost a year since Lizzie had seen Mary. They had so much to catch up on. With Rachel's wedding and their *vader*'s illness, no doubt their chatter would fill an entire afternoon. But Lizzie couldn't wait to get her sister alone to talk about Paul.

No sooner did those thoughts leave her head than the sound of a ruckus came from out in the yard. After wiping her hands on a dish towel, Lizzie followed her *daed* outside, where they found Paul helping her sister and Aaron down from the wagon.

Lizzie took off at a run, meeting her sister halfway

down the walkway. "Mary! I'm so excited that you're finally home." Lizzie let out a squeal of delight as she ran into her arms.

Their *mamm* came out from around back, running so hard, she was out of breath by the time she got there. "It's wonderful to have my *dochdern* together!"

Stepping back, she cocked her head to one side, giving Mary the once-over, observing, "Mary, you are glowing. This can only mean one thing!" their mother exclaimed, her eyes tearing up. "You're going to have a *bobbli*!"

Rubbing a hand over her stomach, Mary took hold of Aaron's arm, pulling him in close. "*Bopplin.* We're having twins."

Mamm's hand flew to her chest. "Twins! This is wonderful news."

"If it's all right, I'd like to get Mary into the house. It was a long trip and she needs to put her feet up," Aaron advised, putting a protective arm around Mary's shoulders.

Mary swatted her *mann*'s arm. "Aaron, I've told you before, I am not an invalid."

"Come along anyway," her *mamm* said, taking Mary's hand and escorting her up the steps.

Lizzie watched as her family moved to the house, leaving her alone beside Paul. Fussing with the front of her apron, she found herself happy to see him. She'd missed him. Lizzie wondered if he felt the same way about her.

"That was nice of you to bring my sister and her *mann* here."

"I had to pick up a furniture order from the workroom at my *vader*'s. There are a few cabinets that I'd finished up before I opened my shop, and the customer is ready to receive them," he explained. "The trip out here was no trouble. That's *gut* news about your sister."

"*Ja.* It is. I'm going to be an *aenti*."

"You're going to make a fine one, at that, *Aenti* Lizzie."

"Oh, my, when you say call me that, it makes the news seem that much more real."

"I have the recipe box you wanted for Rachel and Jacob's wedding gift." He reached around to get the small box from underneath the wagon's seat.

The box looked so tiny in Paul's strong hands. He handed it to her. Lizzie stared down in awe. The cherrywood box had tiny hearts carved into all four sides. On the top were the words *Made with love*. Running her thumb over the smooth wood, Lizzie knew Rachel would get much use out of this.

Raising her eyes, she met Paul's clear gaze. "This is lovely."

"Danke." Nodding at her, he said, "Go ahead and open it."

Carefully she lifted the lid and peered inside to find a white envelope that had been folded in half. "What's this?"

"It's for you," he answered, rocking back on his heels.

Lizzie had never seen him so excited. She didn't

know what to expect, but whatever was inside had Paul beaming. "I can't imagine what this could be."

"Lizzie, just open it up already."

"Okay, okay." Lizzie reached in and removed the envelope.

As she unfolded the paper, she realized it was thicker than it looked. *What on earth?* She broke the seal open and was shocked to find cash inside.

"Paul, what is this? What have you done?"

"Oh, I didn't do anything, Lizzie. It was you. This is from the sale of your first piece of art."

"This can't be. The watercolors have been there for less than a week." She stared at the money in disbelief. Quickly, she thumbed her fingers across the bills. "There must be a hundred dollars in here."

A broad smile stretched across his face. "One hundred and seventy-five dollars, to be exact."

In her excitement over seeing what he'd brought her, Lizzie pushed convention aside and flung herself into his arms. Her entire being vibrated with emotions. This money would help her family at a time when they needed it the most.

"Oh, Paul!" Her voice hitched. "Thank you." She squeezed him tightly.

The air around them seemed to grow still. Lizzie felt Paul's arms wrapped around her. She laid her head against his chest and heard the strong beating of his heart. She couldn't hold back a grin, because hers felt as if it were going to burst from her chest. For this one brief moment she allowed herself to feel safe and loved.

Lizzie pulled back a bit and stared up at him. She saw his powerful love reflected in those beautiful dark eyes. If she'd ever doubted his feelings before, now, in this very instant, Lizzie saw and felt the things he'd been trying for so long to tell her.

"Lizzie… I—"

She yearned to hear him say the words that would change her life. But the only sound she heard was that of a loud tractor engine shattering their moment. Paul dropped his arms at the same time Lizzie stepped out of his reach. Blinking up at him, she wanted to tell him to leave before her *vader* caught them in a compromising situation. But Paul just stood there watching her. She could tell he wasn't going to be moving anytime soon from where he stood.

Worry began to nibble at her conscience. Would he stay there until her *vader* came out of the house to check on them? Would Paul continue to honor their agreement now that she'd made the first sale of her art at his shop? But the biggest question she couldn't get out of her mind was how could she ever have a future with this furniture maker when her family needed a farmer?

Paul's arms felt empty without Lizzie standing in them. He knew that her feelings for him were deepening. She didn't know it, but he'd been watching her grow and change over these past months. He'd been holding out hope that she would come around to selling her art and, after that proved successful, grow to trust him…to love him. Now that those things had happened, she hadn't said that she loved him. But he could see the change in the way she felt about him from the look on her face. She wasn't looking away from him. And he hadn't seen her pull away or turn her face to hide her scar in weeks.

These were all good things and an answer to his many prayers.

Paul could be patient a bit longer. The rest would come. And one day soon he and Lizzie would declare their love for one another.

He heard the sound of Mary's laughter and Aaron joining in.

Then Joseph called out, "Lizzie! Where have you gone off to? Come join the rest of the family to welcome your sister home."

The screen door slapped closed behind the man as Joseph came out onto the porch. "There you are."

He saw them together, and Paul watched the man's eyes narrow in disapproval.

"Come. Come inside," he said, motioning to Lizzie. "Paul, you're welcome to have some pie with us to celebrate Mary's return."

"*Danke* for the offer, Joseph. But I have to get this order delivered." Paul nodded to the cabinets still needed to be unloaded. "I need to be getting on. I'm glad your family is all under one roof again."

"*Ja.* It's a happy day, indeed." The man made a big show of adjusting the straps on his suspenders.

Paul took the hint. He waved to Joseph, then turned to face Lizzie. "I'll look for you at Rachel and Jacob's wedding reception."

"I'd like that. And, Paul?"

"Yes?"

She patted the pocket she'd put the money in. "This is still just between us."

"You can count on it."

"*Gut.* I'll see you at the wedding."

Chapter Eleven

The day of Rachel and Jacob's wedding dawned gray with a cool drizzle. Soon the roads and fields surrounding the Miller farm would be covered with buggies. This was a big day in Miller's Crossing. Rachel and Jacob had a lot of family members who'd be attending, besides their friends and neighbors in the surrounding communities. From what Lizzie had heard, they were expecting almost five hundred people to show up. She'd heard about weddings where over one thousand people came to join in the celebration, so she supposed this wedding might be considered small compared to that.

She imagined if she were to have a wedding of her own, it wouldn't be anywhere near that size. The image of Paul standing tall and handsome flitted through her mind. Lizzie realized she had a long way to go as far as her feelings for him were concerned. These feelings of love were so new and fresh. A part of her wanted to embrace the sensation, while another part of her was so scared by the notion, she didn't know what to do. He'd been so kind to her over these past weeks. She looked at the spot where she'd put the money he'd brought her. The small basket sitting on top of her dresser held the future of her family. She needed to bring him more of her artwork. She decided after the wedding was done that she'd make plans to go into town to his shop.

Aware that it was getting late, Lizzie ran her hands along the front of her best Sunday dress, making sure there wasn't a wrinkle to be seen. She ran a brush through her hair and then took great care to wind it up into a bun at the back of her head. After that she carefully pinned her prayer *kapp* on her head. The rich smell of freshly brewed coffee wafted upstairs. She headed down to join her family for their morning meal.

Her *vader* sat at the head of the kitchen table and looked up as she came into the room. His bushy eyebrows came together. "Getting a late start, aren't you, Lizzie?"

"I'm sorry," she said, heading to the stove to replace his second cup of coffee with some herbal tea.

His last doctor's visit had gone quite well. But he'd been warned about his caffeine. He needed to cut back.

Vader eyed the teapot. "Lizzie, I hope that's not for me."

Turning her head, she looked over her shoulder at him. "And what if it is? You heard what the doctor told you."

"*Ja.* But I will make do with less coffee before I ever switch to *that*."

Resigned that she couldn't change his mind, she set the teapot off to one side on the counter. Mary and Aaron came in to join them. She thought her sister looked a bit pale, so she opened the narrow cabinet next to the stove and pulled out a box of ginger tea bags. After grabbing the teapot, she placed a bag inside and then poured hot water from the kettle over it.

While the tea brewed, she said to her sister, "Come. Sit, Mary. I'm steeping some ginger tea I think might do you some good."

Letting Aaron hold the chair out for her, Mary sat. "*Danke.* These babies are already making their presence known. Can you get me some dry toast? Sometimes that helps with this morning sickness, too."

Mamm walked behind Lizzie, carrying a slice of toast on a white plate. "This should do the trick."

Grabbing a cup of tea for herself, Lizzie joined the family at the table. Her *vader* bowed his head and began the morning prayer.

"Lord, *danke* for this day. *Danke* for the food on our table. We are grateful for the bounty You've bestowed upon us, not only in our food, but in our growing family. May You bring blessings upon Rachel and Jacob on what I know will turn out to be a fine day. Continue to guide us all in the way You see fit."

"Amen," Lizzie whispered.

Paul stood with a group of his friends, watching the buggies roll into the yard. For over an hour he'd been waiting, looking for the right one. The problem was the buggies for the most part looked the same and, in a crowd as large as this one, it was going to be hard for him to pick out Joseph Miller's. The drizzle from this morning had given way to a sunshine-filled afternoon. The dark clouds had dissipated, leaving behind a sky as blue as the ocean.

From his vantage point Paul took in the large food tent placed in front of the barn. Alongside that was a rented food trailer. The smell of the wedding *roascht* filled the air. The roasted chicken and vegetables would continue to cook until it was time to serve the throng of people. Then the tables would be laden with the chickens, potatoes, carrots, celery and wedding cakes and pies.

Ben jostled his arm, bringing Paul's attention back to the line of buggies along the roadway.

"I think that's the one you've been waiting for." He nodded toward the Millers' vehicle.

Paul caught a glimpse of Lizzie through the window of the back seat of the buggy top and gave a wave. Paul watched as Joseph followed the direction of one the neighbor boys, driving almost all the way down to the end of the second row before finding an opening to park in. Joseph helped his wife and then Mary down from the buggy. Lizzie came next. The family came toward him, and he saw the women carrying their wedding gifts. Paul felt a bit of pride well up inside knowing that Lizzie was carrying the recipe box he'd made.

"Good afternoon, Paul," Lizzie's *vader* said, stepping out in front of his family to greet him. "We've a fine day for this celebration."

"*Ja.* That we do, sir." Paul's gaze met Lizzie's. He couldn't help but notice how pretty she looked today. She wore a dress he'd seen her wear to church services. The light blue color matched her eyes. Her honey-colored hair was up in a neat bun, underneath her prayer *kapp.*

"There's a lot of people here," Lizzie commented. "And even a few *Englischers.*"

Paul saw the shadows of wariness in her eyes. She stepped back. His instincts made him want to reach out to her, to tell her not to worry, that he'd protect her from whatever she was afraid of. She ran her hand up along the right side of her face, her fingers skimming the scarred area. She didn't need to hide herself from others. He wanted to take her in his arms and comfort her. He needed to assure her that he'd always protect her, no matter what.

Except, if he were to be honest with himself, he knew he couldn't always be there to protect her. The one day she'd needed him the most, he'd been too late. Too late to save his friend David and too late to keep Lizzie from harm's way. Paul vowed he would continue to do his best to give Lizzie the life she so deserved.

Out of the corner of his eye, he caught Lizzie's *vader* watching them. Paul gave Joseph a nod and then started to walk toward the festivities. He continued to say hello to those he knew, but his attention never wavered from Lizzie. He wanted to grab hold of her hand. But he knew it wouldn't be proper to display his affections in public. His thoughts filled with the memory of their time together up on Clymer Hill. The day had been perfect for a picnic, and watching her paint, he'd been amazed at the talent she possessed.

They entered the wedding tent, where Paul joined his family. Lizzie's family sat on the benches in the row across from them. They all settled in for the three-hour ceremony.

The congregation began to sing the opening hymns as Rachel and Jacob were led off to a room with the bishop and ministers for their time of *Abroth*, admonition and encouragement. After they returned, the bishop preached a sermon about love and faith. When it came time for the Bible reading, Paul quieted, preparing his mind and heart to hear the words.

After Rachel and Jacob came forward and answered their vow qucstions, there came the closing prayer and then they were pronounced *Frau* and *Mann*. After the service Paul ran to catch up with Lizzie but saw her being swept away by Sadie and a few other women. She laughed at something Sadie said. It warmed his heart to see her so happy.

He joined his *bruders* under the branches of a large oak tree. Jebediah Troyer, one of the church elders, came up to him.

"How is your business faring, Paul?"

"The shop is doing better than I anticipated," Paul answered, fighting the urge to rub his hand across the back of his neck. He knew the elders had been watching the situation between him and his *vader*.

"I'm glad to hear that. You keep up the good work. I know your family will come around to your way of thinking eventually. We are praying for that."

Paul was surprised that the elders felt this way. Normally they sided with the head of the family in situations like this.

"But if it doesn't work out that way, you will return to your *vader*'s shop."

He knew better than to speak openly at a wedding about his thoughts on the Burkholder Furniture Store. Paul thanked the elder and turned as Jacob and Rachel caught his attention. The bride, wearing a new white *kapp*, and the groom, with his wide-brimmed hat—signaling that they were now a married couple—wandered around the masses of people. They tapped the single young men and women on the shoulder, pairing them off for the meal. When they came to him, Paul shook his head. The only woman he wanted to share his meal with was Lizzie. He wouldn't feel right turning down their pairing, but hoped he wouldn't have to be put in the position of declining.

Rachel bubbled with happiness. "Paul, Jacob and I want you to come with us."

Taking hold of his arm, she tugged him along to the grassy clearing, where another dining tent had been erected. "I can't..."

"You don't even know who we've picked for you," Jacob said, slapping him on the back.

He ducked his head and entered the tent. Lanterns hung from the sides of the tent and lining the tables cast a warm glow, lighting the way. The air smelled of the wedding *roascht* and wildflowers. There were Queen Anne's lace, lavender and fern fronds filling the dozens of canning jars. Outside the tent, the *kinder* chased the fireflies, hoping to catch a few to put in their empty jars. His gaze swung back into the tent filled with young couples. Some looking happier than others about their handpicked tablemates.

Then he saw her. Standing on the other side. She had her hands folded together in front of her. Her head was a bit downcast. At this very moment Paul wanted to do away with this silly tradition of walk-a-mile among the *youngies*. Unfortunately this wasn't his wedding.

"Come." Rachel beamed up at him.

She led him right to Lizzie.

"Paul!"

He heard the relief in her voice and watched as some of the tension fell from her face. He cocked his head to one side, saying, "Lizzie. It looks like we've been paired off."

"Ja."

Taking her by the elbow, Paul led her to an open spot at the long row of tables. Leaning down, he said in a soft voice, "I've been wondering where you got off to."

"Sadie and I went inside the *haus* to leave our wedding gifts. I was hoping to avoid this."

He chuckled. "Me, too. At least they put us together. I would have been angry if you'd been put with another man."

"I wouldn't have accepted," she assured him.

"I'm glad we'll be together."

"I've played at this game plenty of times before, Paul. And mostly I've been alone or left to eat with my parents." She gave a shrug, adding, "It's no big deal, but I like this go-round much better."

Paul felt a tightening in his chest. He hadn't meant his words to be hurtful. In all the years he'd stood by and watched Lizzie grow from a young girl into a young woman, it hadn't occurred to him the pain she'd been enduring. In a society that valued marriages and family, it was difficult to be single.

"I'm sorry if I sounded insensitive."

"You weren't being insensitive. You were being honest. I like honesty."

The tent filled with more couples. Pretty soon the seats across from them and on either side of them became occupied. Some of the people he recognized, and others he'd never seen before, as they came from neighboring church districts. He watched as, one after the other, their tablemates averted their eyes from Lizzie. He felt her stiffen when a particular young man outright made a sour face in her direction.

Seeing firsthand what she'd been enduring for years sickened him. He thought he might have to ask the stranger to leave the table. Lizzie must have been sensing his thoughts, because she gave him a warning look and a quick shake of her head.

"I could ask him to leave."

"*Nee*. Don't bother. I'm fine, really."

Still he saw the hurt in her eyes and watched as she started to shield her face with one hand. He wasn't having any of this. This was a festive and joyous day, and she deserved to enjoy herself. Grabbing hold of her hand, he pulled her off the seat.

"Come on."

Leaving her napkin behind, she left the tent with him. He found them a quiet spot at the edge of the yard, away from prying eyes.

Tugging her hand out of his grip, she stood still. He suddenly realized his abrupt actions might not have helped matters.

"Paul, it's all right. I'm used to that sort of thing."

"You shouldn't have to be used to it." He scuffed the toe of his boot along the ground in front of him. "I never understood until today."

"Few people do. But I don't want people to like me or want to be with me because they feel sorry for me, either." Folding her arms across her chest, she meandered around to the other side of the pine tree they'd stopped at. "Don't ever feel sorry for me."

He heard the hurt and a bit of determination in her voice and felt like the worst kind of the worst.

Laying his hand against the rough bark, he dragged it along as he joined her on the other side. Up until this point it had been a beautiful day. He didn't want to ruin it with the silly notion that he was sure Lizzie was thinking, that somehow he was spending time with her out of pity. He stopped moving when he came to her. She had her face turned downward, her eyes half-closed. Paul could see the scar on her cheek, except to him it was no longer a scar.

It was a part of the woman he loved.

"Elizabeth Miller, I don't feel sorry for you. You are one of the bravest, most courageous people I know. I had no idea, all these years, what you must have suffered at the hands of strangers, at the hands of those who know you," he added, thinking about the words her *vader* had said to him that day, months ago, on their front porch.

Joseph had been wrong to assume that Lizzie couldn't find love on her own. Saying that his daughter's appearance would keep her from finding a husband had been downright wrong.

Oh, Paul knew the man had said those things out of desperation, but still Lizzie deserved so much better than that. From the distance came the sound of singing. He gazed down at Lizzie, rubbing his thumb over her chin.

"Do you want to try again for something to eat?"

"*Nee.* I'm not hungry."

He tipped his head to the side, "Lizzie, don't let them keep you away."

"I'm not. I had a snack when Sadie and I dropped our gifts off, before the ceremony started."

"You're not just telling me that to make me feel better?"

"And what if I am?" she admitted.

"Well, I'd be sad that we didn't get to share Rachel and Jacob's wedding feast together." Pushing away from the tree, he offered, "Let's go see if there's any food left."

At that very moment Paul's *vader* approached them with two men flanking him. Paul recognized Silas Yoder, and from the looks of the other man, who was dressed in a white collared shirt and tan pants, Paul knew him to be an *Englischer*.

"Here you are! I want you to meet someone." His *vader* took hold of his arm, taking him away from Lizzie.

"This is Kurt Reynolds, a friend of Jacob's *vader*. He went by your shop today."

The man pushed a pair of sunglasses on top of his head, saying, "Yes, I stopped by on my way out here for the wedding. I didn't realize you'd be closed on a Thursday."

"*Ja*. We close our businesses on wedding days," Paul explained.

He didn't want to talk business. He wanted to spend time with Lizzie. She'd stepped off to the side to let him carry on this conversation.

"I've been hearing great things about your furniture. I also heard that you have a limited selection of watercolors."

Lizzie gasped.

Paul covered her reaction by taking the gentleman by the arm and leading him farther away from her. He didn't miss his *vader*'s raised eyebrows. Clearly he was surprised to hear Paul was selling art in addition to his furniture. Perhaps if the man gave Paul's venture more attention, he wouldn't have to be hearing about this. Paul tried his best to keep his frustration out of this conversation. Besides, this day was supposed to be about happiness and love, not business. He wanted to be with Lizzie.

He wanted to tell her he loved her. Today would have been a perfect day to broach the idea of a real courtship between them. First, though, he wanted to tell her everything about the day David died. Because deep in his heart Paul knew they couldn't begin any sort of a life together until the past was laid to rest.

Suddenly he noticed that she was pulling away from him. He saw her walking off to meet Sadie Fischer. Paul started to call to her, but she turned to him, tilted her head ever so slightly and smiled.

He smiled back. The moment was interrupted by the sound of the *Englischer*'s voice.

"Would it be all right if I stopped by your furniture shop tomorrow?" he asked.

Paul snapped his head around to give the future customer his attention. "*Ja*, *ja*. You can come by tomorrow. That would be *gut*."

"Good. I'll see you then."

The man held his hand out, and Paul shook it. Over the top of the man's head, he watched Lizzie join Sadie, say something in her ear and then walk off with her.

What could they possibly be talking about?

Chapter Twelve

"Lizzie! I've been looking all over for you. Do you want to come join in the singing with me?" Sadie came bounding across the lawn to meet up with her.

Her friend's bright personality always made her feel better. At some weddings, hymns would be sung after the ceremony while the presents were being opened or as an activity late into the night. And normally she enjoyed singing the hymns, but not tonight. Paul had invited her to go with him and they'd been interrupted. She found that she didn't want to go with anyone else.

"Would you mind taking a walk with me to the cake tables instead?" she asked Sadie.

"I've been seeing some delicious slices of cake being passed around. I hope there is at least some left."

Leaving the men to talk business, Lizzie fell into step alongside her friend.

"I feel like it's been days and days since we've seen each other."

Nodding her head, Lizzie agreed. "*Ja*. I've been busy feeding a lot of workers who are helping with the harvest on the farm, and working on my watercolors. And my sister came home with news that she's having twins."

"Congratulations. You're going to be an *aenti*. I'm so happy for you and your family," Sadie said, giving her a warm hug. Then, taking a step back, she added, "I've heard some other news."

"What might that be?"

"That you have been spending a lot of time with Paul lately."

Lizzie nibbled her lower lip. Of course it would be silly to think that in a town this size anything could be kept quiet.

"Tell me this means the two of you are in a courtship." Sadie clapped her hands together.

"We are not. But..."

"Oh, but what, Lizzie? There should be no buts allowed when it comes to you and Paul being together." In her exuberance Sadie spun around. "You deserve to be happy."

Lizzie couldn't agree more. Laughing at Sadie, she commented, "I wish I had even half of your confidence."

Sadie stilled. "Do not be fooled, my friend. There are things that continue to elude me."

"Like what?"

"Like why you insist on taking so long to get to the cake tent."

Sadie linked her arm through Lizzie's. They

laughed and chattered the rest of the way across the yard, finally entering the area where tables covered with white tablecloths were laden with platters of cakes and cookies. After picking up a slice of cake with blue frosting, she followed Sadie back outside. They found an empty space at one of the tables.

They dug into their cakes. When they were finished eating, Sadie asked, "Do you think your *vader* would allow you to be courted by Paul?"

Lizzie shrugged. "I'm not sure. These feelings are still so new to me. And I haven't told Paul how I feel yet."

"You need to do this. Soon. Paul is a fine man and he could be snatched up by someone else," Sadie warned, waving her fork in front of her face. "Maybe Paul will get his letter to prove his good standing in the church from the bishop and then he can ask for your *daed*'s blessing."

She knew Paul had been baptized and that getting the *Zeugnis* was merely a formality. "I don't know. I think you're getting ahead of yourself." Lizzie tried not to panic over the idea of Sadie even suggesting that Paul might find another woman.

"I've known for a long time that Paul is the right one for you." Poking the end of her fork at her, Sadie, added, "Trust what is in your heart."

Lizzie thought that might be easier said than done. Sadie wanted to wander around the wedding, visiting with friends and family, but Lizzie didn't feel up to it.

"Go ahead, Sadie. I'll wait for Paul."

"If you're sure."

Lizzie gave her a nod. "I am. Now run along."

Sadie had always been the more social one between the two of them. Even as young schoolgirls, once they'd gone out to the playground, Sadie had been the one to round everyone up for games, while Lizzie had lingered on the edge of the circle. She didn't mind that her friend went off to socialize. Lizzie enjoyed sitting here, watching everyone around her. Knowing that Paul wasn't far away. He'd be coming back to find her soon. And if her guess were right, he'd be bringing news of a big sale with him.

Lizzie had a feeling that the *Englischer* wanted to purchase some of Paul's furniture. She didn't mind waiting, though after a while she did tire of sitting alone and decided to walk about the grounds, stopping to say hello to her brother-in-law Aaron's mother, Sara Yoder, who was busy talking to some friends. Lizzie paused to listen to their conversation. They were discussing how large the gathering was and how happy they were for Rachel and Jacob.

Though Sara Yoder wouldn't be discussing Lizzie's sister Mary's impending birth, Lizzie knew the news was a joyous time for both of their families.

As Sara Yoder and the other women went on about the wedding, Lizzie believed in her heart that this is what the Amish community was best at, welcoming new family members into the fold. Lizzie knew that, no matter what, she would never want to live anywhere other than right here. No matter what happened between her and Paul, her home would always be in Miller's Crossing.

Leaving the women's circle, she walked up a small rise, turning around at the top. Below her lay the wedding. Buggies lined the back field in rows, three deep. The canvas walls of the tents had been rolled down to help keep the bugs out. Through the plastic window cutouts, she could see the lovely lanterns all lit up. It looked so pretty. She tried to imagine what it would be like to have a grand wedding day such as this for herself. Lizzie knew it would all be too much for her.

She wouldn't mind a simple wedding ceremony with her family and close friends attending. As the singing continued and the *kinders* ran in circles on the lawn, Lizzie allowed herself to dream about her wedding day. Of course the *mann* she'd pick would be Paul Burkholder. Not only was he a *gut* friend, but he was kind and caring. Now that she thought about it, he'd always been a part of her life. And she couldn't imagine her life without him.

She wandered down near the barn, with the fireflies buzzing around her. Lizzie let out a sigh. There must be a million stars shining in the sky tonight. She had to find Paul to show him this glory. Suddenly she was startled by a sound coming from the bushes.

Paul walked toward her out of the darkness.

"Oh, it's you, Paul. Did you have a *gut* meeting?"

"I did." He came closer and put his hands on her shoulders.

She felt his strength and warmth emanate through his hands, and she felt his...love. They stayed like that for a few minutes, until Paul let go. She gave him a questioning look, wondering what this was all about.

"The man, Mr. Reynolds, he wants to come by the shop tomorrow. He's interested in the dining room set. You know, the one I've had on display since I opened?"

She nodded.

"And, as you know, he's heard about your art. As it turns out he knows the person who bought the first piece. I guess they've been raving about you."

"Me?" Lizzie felt panic rising. No one could know she was the artist. No one.

Paul immediately grabbed her hands, holding them in his. "I promise no one except for myself and Sadie know you're the artist. What I should have said is they are raving about the anonymous artist."

She breathed a sigh of relief. "That's better. Well, I'm pleased this day has turned out well for you and for me."

"The day has been better than okay, Lizzie. With the sale of the dining set and your artwork, some of the burdens are being lifted from us and our families. I've been thinking this could be a good time to reconsider our relationship."

The expression on his face made her laugh.

"You're joking!"

"Actually I'm quite serious about this. I'd give you more time to think about this, but I think you've had enough time already."

"Not even courting me yet, and here you are, bossing me around."

"I would never." He picked up her hands, brought them to his lips and kissed the top of each one. "I've waited a long time for us to court and I need everything to be just right."

Her eyes widened. Was he going to kiss her on the lips? Tonight she'd be perfectly content with the affection he'd been showing her. But the thought of his mouth on hers made her feel like nothing else on earth. Not even the joy she took from her paintings and watching the sunset could compare. He came closer, his arms grazing hers. She looked up into his eyes and once again felt overwhelmed by the love she saw there.

She so wanted to have the courage to pour her heart out to him, to say the words he most wanted to hear. But she didn't want to give her heart to him only to have her *vader* take all of this away if he didn't approve of a courtship between them.

Then he said, "I'd like to come by your house tomorrow. I have something I need to tell you."

"*Ja.* I'd like that," she answered as a tiny bit of doubt managed to creep back in.

Lizzie did her best to fight off any uncertainty about their relationship, deciding that loving someone could be a hard and sometimes unpredictable part of life.

"The night is getting on. Let me get you back to your parents."

Lizzie let him hold her hand as they walked back to the cake tent. She tipped her head back one last time, wanting to memorize the beauty of the night sky. The stars sparkling way up in the heavens gave her hope. A star shot across the inky sky.

"Paul! Did you see that?"

"I did."

She squeezed his hand, looking forward to what tomorrow might bring.

Sitting on the edge of his bed, Paul bowed his head in morning prayer. Afterward he rose, took his hat from the peg behind his bedroom door and walked downstairs to the kitchen. His *mamm* stood at the stove, stirring a pot of what smelled like bread and butter pickles. The tangy odor tickled his nose.

Looking up at him, she said, "Good morning, Paul. Do you have another busy day planned?"

"I do." He didn't explain further.

After pouring himself a cup of coffee, he leaned a hip against the counter while he sipped the dark brew.

"Your *vader* tells me that your shop is doing well. He said an *Englischer* is buying one of your dining room sets."

"*Ja*, he is."

Setting the stainless steel spoon on the spoon rest, his *mamm* turned to give him her full attention.

"This rift between you and your *vader*... It's going to end soon."

He couldn't tell if that were her wishful thinking or a command to make it happen. Either way he planned on dealing with his *vader* later today. When it came to stubbornness, the two of them were evenly matched. Knowing this estrangement had not been easy on his *mamm* made him realize he needed to fix the situation. Soon.

But first things first.

His *mamm* ended the silence. "Let me make you some eggs before you head out."

Putting his coffee cup in the sink, he declined his *mamm*'s offer to cook him breakfast. "*Danke, Mamm*, but I've got a lot going on this morning."

She put her hands on her hips, giving him a stern look. "You're going to skip breakfast? You'll be starving by noontime."

He dropped a kiss on her forehead and he said, "I'll be fine, *Mamm*."

Putting his hat on, Paul headed out the door. He went into the barn, and after hitching the mare to the buggy, climbed up into the seat and started out to the Miller house. Though he'd rehearsed in his head what he wanted to say to her a hundred times, to actually tell her the things in his heart and on his mind made him very nervous.

He'd never felt this way before; the sensation that his stomach was all tied up in knots had him shifting on the seat. He prayed one more time, this time asking *Gott* for strength. Taking a deep breath, he blew it out as he made the final turn into the Millers' drive. He spotted Lizzie on the front porch, sitting next to her sister. Lizzie had been so happy when she'd told him that her sister would be having twins. One day he wanted to have a family of his own.

He wanted to have a family with Lizzie.

Stepping down from the buggy, he looped the leather reins over the hitching post next to the house.

Squaring his shoulder, he climbed the steps to greet Lizzie and Mary.

"Paul Burkholder, did you know my sister has a talent as an artist?"

He looked at Lizzie, who shook her head.

"I may have heard a rumor. Good morning, ladies."

He noticed a slight blush creeping over Lizzie's delicate cheekbones as she acknowledged him. "Good morning, Paul."

Dropping her brush into a canning jar filled with water that looked as if it had been clouded with several colors, she turned to look up at him, saying, "Aaron is out in the fields with *Vader*, and *Mamm* went into the village with our neighbor Mrs. Meyer to pick up some prenatal vitamins for Mary. I decided to put some more work in on the picture I started a few weeks ago."

He walked in front of Mary and stood behind Lizzie, looking over her shoulder. His heart clenched when he saw the image of the barn. The fine lines of the building set against the backdrop of the summer field tugged at him. The barn doors were cracked open just enough to see the darkness inside the building. He noticed that Lizzie had added in a lilac bush on the right side. Glancing over his shoulder, he noticed there wasn't one there. It struck him then. She'd painted this scene as she'd remembered the setting from that long-ago day. With each stroke of her brush, Lizzie managed to pull a peaceful beauty out of a day marred with tragedy.

He was in awe of her talent.

"Hey. Can you take a break?" Paul inquired.

"Mary, will you be okay if Paul and I take a walk?" Lizzie asked.

"Actually, if it's all right with both of you, I'd like to take Lizzie for a ride back up to Clymer Hill."

His mention of their picnic spot brought a sudden smile to Lizzie's lips.

"Let me put these things back in my room," Lizzie said, gathering the painting and her art supplies.

As soon as Lizzie went inside, Mary said to Paul, "I need you to be careful where Lizzie is concerned. She's been through a lot in her short life. I don't want to see her hurt again, Paul."

"I would never hurt her."

"I understand. But since there is no official courtship between you, you must know how fragile she can be." Mary shifted her weight in the rocking chair.

"Do you need me to get anything for you?" he offered.

"I'm fine, *danke*. One more thing. My sister has led a very sheltered life. Even in the short time that I've been home, I've seen the changes in her. Changes for the *gut*. Please don't do anything to ruin that."

Paul would never do anything to intentionally hurt Lizzie. He knew that Mary meant well, still it bothered him that she would think that he was the sort of man who would lead a woman on and then walk away. If Paul had his way, he would never leave Lizzie. Ever.

Chapter Thirteen

As Paul drove them to their special place at Clymer Hill, he thought about what Mary had said to him. He, too, had seen the change in Lizzie. While part of it might be due to their changing relationship, he wanted to believe the happiness and confidence starting to grow in Lizzie had come from within her. He parked the buggy, raising his eyebrows in worry. He hoped bringing her here would be the right thing.

Helping her down from the buggy, Paul didn't think he had the strength to talk about David's death. In order to give her the love he had, Paul needed to tell her everything. Digging deep in his soul, he called upon his faith in *Gott* to help as he walked hand in hand with the woman he loved. They made their way over to sit on the bench situated on a grassy knoll overlooking Miller's Crossing.

She tipped her head to the sky, letting the sunlight bathe her in warmth. Paul smiled as he gazed at her. He knew she'd no idea of how pretty she was. They were taught at a very young age that thinking of one's appearance, other than cleanliness, was considered shallow and not serving the Lord. Lizzie was as far from shallow as a person could get. He rubbed his thumb across the top of her hand. She turned to give him a small smile.

"Lizzie, I..." He stopped himself from saying the last two words: *love you*. With all his being, he loved her. But before he could say those words, he needed to confess his sin.

Nervously he looked out over the vista, watching a hawk circling above the field, searching for its next prey. The bird flapped its wings once and then let the breeze carry it over the field. The bird soared higher and higher, until it was just a speck in the sky.

Keeping his eyes focused on the horizon, he said, "Lizzie, I want to talk about the day David died."

She said nothing, and Paul let the silence hang between them. Why did life have to be filled with such pain? he wondered. When still she didn't respond, he faced her so he could see all of her. The happiness he'd seen in her eyes a short time ago was gone. Her skin looked ashen, and her mouth was downturned, but it was the look in her eyes that shattered his soul.

The light blue color had turned a dark and stormy shade. Tears glistened at their corners. Lizzie pulled away from him. Her body stiffening as her hand slid out of his grasp. Paul's hand felt cold and empty without hers in it. Memories from that day flooded his mind. He closed his eyes, seeing those images again...

It was as if time had stood still and he was that thirteen-year-old boy again, on the cusp of becoming a man. At the time of the accident, he'd been helping his daed *finish up a cabinet when they'd heard the sound of the bell tolling. Three rings sounded in quick succession, followed by a short pause and then three more.*

He rushed to the doorway, calling out, "Daed! *There's trouble!"*

"Ja! *Clancy Yoder stopped by here a few minutes ago. There's been an accident over at Joseph Miller's farm."*

Paul's stomach clenched. He was supposed to be out playing with his friends David and Lizzie Miller, but at the last minute he'd been asked to help finish up a furniture order for the Englisch *family down the road. Catching up to his* vader, *who was already in their buggy, Paul hitched himself up on the seat beside him. The buggy sped onto the roadway, where they joined a dozen other worried neighbors who'd heard the alarm.*

When they reached the Miller farm, a line of black buggies were already crowding both sides of the driveway. Jumping from the seat, he and his daed *hurried along with everyone else, heading toward the barn.*

Running as fast as he could, he pumped his arms and legs harder and harder until his lungs burned. Neighbors shouted as he bumped into them. He didn't care; he had to get to the barn. He elbowed his way through the group of men blocking the large double-

hung white doors. Once inside he paused and bent over at the waist, trying to catch his breath. Gulping in the dust-filled air, he coughed. He raised his head, wiped his hand over his mouth and hurried toward the men who stood huddled around a small body.

A brown-booted foot poking out from beneath a loose pile of hay. David. No! Paul's chest tightened. The rest of his friend's body was twisted at an odd angle at the bottom of a stack of tall hay bales. As he moved closer, he heard sobbing. A pool of blood lay beneath David Miller's head. He fisted his hand against his mouth to keep from crying out...

Paul swiped his hand over his eyes, feeling the prick of the tears well up behind his eyelids. The memory still made him choke up. He swallowed hard, feeling the same panic.

Finally he said, "Lizzie, on that day, after I saw David and I couldn't find you, I thought you might be..."

He couldn't bring himself to finish the sentence. He pulled in a deep breath. His heart was racing, and his stomach muscles were clenching at the memories flooding his mind. Memories he tried so hard to forget. He felt her hand on his, and some of the warmth returned.

"I had searched for you, but it was so hard to see through the groups of neighbors who had come to help. I remember a tall man stopping me. Blocking my path. 'This is no place for a young boy,' the man said."

Paul blinked again. "I remember trying to push past him. I called out to you."

"I don't remember much from that day, Paul. I am so very sorry."

"Ethel Yoder told me to go outside and wait with the others." He could still feel the coolness of the woman's hand where she'd touched his arm.

"I asked her where you were. She kept telling me to leave. And then I finally saw you…"

He remembered sidestepping around the woman. He wasn't leaving until he found Lizzie. Time stood still as the crowd parted. There, a few feet away from her brother, lay Lizzie, her head propped up against the sharp edge of a plow blade, her white prayer kapp *lopsided on her head. Light brown hair hung down on her shoulders, matted together with moisture. Paul wrung his hands together.*

There was a large gash that covered her face, and someone was applying a cloth to stop the bleeding.

Blinking hard, Paul banished the image. He turned to looked at Lizzie. Right here, right now, right this very minute. She didn't even come close to resembling that little girl. She sat here, next to him, with her tear-streaked face, and he thought she looked beautiful. He felt her anguish and wanted to take it all away.

Lizzie's heart felt as if it were breaking into a million pieces. The hurt and pain welled up from somewhere deep inside.

"Why are you doing this now? Why are you ruining this beautiful moment?" she pleaded.

Fresh pain tore through her heart, searing her soul like an open wound. Her head throbbed. She touched the scar on her face, feeling the pain all over again. "Why, Paul?"

"I know how hard this is to hear. But we've been going round and round all these years, avoiding talking about your brother. Talking about our part in the day. We need to go through this pain in order to come out on the other side, healed."

He clutched her hands, his eyes darkening. "I need to be healed, and I know you want that, too."

She sobbed, wanting to run away. The tears rolled down her face. Even though she felt the warmth from the sun on her skin, shivers raced down her spine. He put his hand on her back, covering the exact spot, giving her strength and hope.

"I wasn't supposed to be out in the barn at all. I don't remember much about that time, but I do remember waking up in the hospital and my *daed* being angry with me. He said he'd told me not to go out there to play. I don't understand why I went against his wishes. If I'd listened to him, David might still be alive."

"Lizzie. I was supposed to be there, too. I told David I'd come over. We were going to climb the hay bales. This is as much my fault as it is yours."

Lizzie didn't know what to make of all of this. She knew that *Gott* would never give them more than they could handle. She laid her head against Paul's shoulder, feeling his strength.

"Maybe the fault doesn't lie with either of us.

Maybe it was nothing more than an accident that no one could have prevented." She remembered now how impulsive David had always been. He'd been the one to swing from the rope in the tree in the backyard. He'd been the one to ride his bike as fast as he could down the long hills, while she and Mary had looked on.

Even at that young age, David had been a risk-taker, while Lizzie had always been the one to stand there watching him.

Finally she said, "We don't know how things would have turned out if you'd been there. No one knows. All the times you came by my parents' *haus*, all those years and all those visits—was it because you felt guilty?"

She didn't think she could take it if he said yes, because that could mean only one thing: that this relationship was his way of making things up to her for David's death.

"At first I came because I was so worried about you. And then, *ja*. I guess I had a lot of guilt. I felt terrible that your *vader* was left without a son."

Lizzie swallowed.

"Then I knew we shared something more." Cupping her face between his hands, he tipped her head back, his gaze capturing hers.

Lizzie's breathing picked up. The look in his eyes began to change, going from hurt and pain to hope.

She felt the calluses on the pads of his thumbs as he stroked her jaw.

"I want to kiss you, Lizzie," he whispered. "Would that be all right?"

She nodded.

He lowered his head and gently touched his lips to hers.

He raised his head, resting his forehead against hers. "I'm sorry. That was too bold of me."

"*Nee.* The time was right for our first kiss."

He looked at her with an intensity she'd never seen before. It might be too soon to express his feelings to her, but Paul couldn't hold them back any longer.

"I love you, Lizzie. With all my heart and soul, I love you."

Tears sprang to her eyes again. "Paul." Her voice hitched with emotion, knowing that once she said the words, she couldn't take them back. Her heart blossomed as she spoke. "I love you, too."

His smile stretched from ear to ear. "I can't believe I'm hearing you say those words. Lizzie, you mean so very much to me. And I know there's still so much to be done to make our courtship work."

"Like getting my *vader*'s permission. He still wants a son-in-law to take over the farm." She reached out to touch his face, smiling when she felt the light stubble beneath her fingertips.

This was the first time she'd touched his face. He felt like warmth and light and love.

As he covered her hand with his, she felt the corners of his mouth turn up.

Then he replied to her comment about her *vader.* "Maybe once Joseph sees how well your paintings are doing and the fact that I can support a family with my furniture store, he'll come around."

Lizzie wanted to believe him. She knew that her *vader* could be very stubborn when it came to what he wanted in his family and for his farm. She also wanted to believe that he would like to see his daughter happy.

Happy. She let the feeling sink in. For the first time in as long as she could remember, Lizzie felt not just happy, but happiness.

Gathering her in his arms, Paul pulled her close. "Oh, Lizzie, I love you so much. But I think we need to be getting back. I don't want to worry your parents."

"That wouldn't be a good thing to do," she agreed.

When he started to help her up off the bench, she put her hand over his chest, stilling his movement. Beneath her fingers, his heart beat at a strong, steady rate. She closed her eyes, imagining their life together. Maybe they could have one of the smaller farms off in the distance. Perhaps there would be children. Lizzie knew if they were blessed with a son, she would name him after her brother and pray that he wasn't as impulsive.

"Elizabeth Miller. When we return to your home, I'm going to ask your *vader* if I may court you. It's time to make this official."

Lizzie's heart swelled.

He kissed her forehead. "Let's get you home."

Lizzie wanted the ride home to last forever. She wanted to savor the moment when Paul had told her he loved her for as long as she could. But as soon as he turned the buggy into the driveway, she knew trouble had come their way.

Chapter Fourteen

She saw an unfamiliar car parked in front of the house. The blue SUV looked out of place next to the buggy. There was a man standing in front of the driver's-side door. Her *vader* was standing in front of the stranger who towered a good foot over his height. His face was red as a beet and he was pointing at the man, then pointing toward the road. Lizzie had never seen her *vader* this angry.

Lizzie grabbed hold of Paul's arm. "Hurry!"

"Oh, no," he muttered.

"Do you recognize the man?"

"*Ja.* He's the one who stopped by the wedding to ask about buying some of my furniture. I can't imagine what he's doing at your house."

The buggy jerked as Paul pulled the mare to a sudden stop. He jumped down, leaving Lizzie to catch up to him.

"Joseph! What's going on here?" Paul asked, stepping between the two men.

"This man—" her *vader* pointed a finger at the man "—he came out here asking about some art. I told him more than once we don't have any art here. I don't know what he's carrying on about."

Lizzie's heart sank like a rock. This couldn't be happening. How did this man find out who she was or where she lived? She cast a questioning glance toward Paul, who only shook his head in confusion.

"I went by your shop today, Paul. Your brother was there. After I bought the dining room set, I took a look at the watercolors. My wife loves to collect Amish artwork. The ones you have would be perfect for her collection. Ben, he told me the art was limited editions, and there were no artist markings. But then he looked at the one I was interested in and said he recognized the scene. He pointed me in this direction. I'm so sorry. I didn't mean to cause any trouble."

"I don't know what this man is talking about. He's been describing our fields perfectly. I don't understand." Her *vader*'s voice quieted as he looked to Paul for answers.

She caught the *Englischer* staring at her, seeing the scar on her face. His glance collided with hers, and Lizzie saw him grimace. Quickly he looked away from her. The old insecurities came rushing back in like an out-of-control tidal wave, leaving her emotions shaking.

She never should have left the farm.

Doing her best to hide the scar, she lowered her head, taking a step forward. Knowing it would be wrong to keep the truth from her *vader*. She had never wanted him to find out, but the truth always had a way of coming out. She glanced over at Paul, thinking, *How could this have happened?* He was supposed to protect her. He'd promised her no one would find out. And now Lizzie had to face her family. She had to face the one person who had doubted her for the past decade. The man who would never forgive her for David's death. She bit back a sob, unable to think clearly.

"I have something to tell you, *Vader*," she said, her voice barely above a whisper.

All her hopes and dreams for a future with Paul came crashing down. But she couldn't bear to keep this from her *vader*, even if she'd done it for all the right reasons; he deserved to know what she'd been doing.

"You need to tell us what, *Dochder*?" *Vader* asked, as his face turned even redder.

"*I'm* the one who paints the watercolors Paul sells."

Silence descended on the group. Tension snapped in the air like lightning. Lizzie kept her eyes downcast. She couldn't look at her *vader*. And she didn't want to see Paul. All the things they'd just confessed to each other…all the love they'd declared…it meant nothing now. If Paul couldn't protect her, then no one could. Just like the day of the accident. The cold reality hit her with such a jolt, she almost fell to the ground. Summoning what little strength she had left, she raised her eyes to meet her *vader*'s gaze. She felt foolish thinking that selling her art to help out the family would work. Shame at her deception shook her to her soul.

It broke her heart to see his disappointment in her.

"Go to the house. Now."

Gulping back the sobs, she turned, doing as she was told. Entering the house, she heard the car door slam shut and then the stranger driving off. She heard her *vader* order Paul off the property.

But not before she heard Paul's voice defending her. "She did this to help your family, sir."

The screen door banged shut behind her as she fell into her *mamm*'s arms, sobbing uncontrollably.

"There, there, *Dochder*. It's going to be all right. I promise." Her *mamm* led her upstairs to her bedroom, where she helped Lizzie lie down on the bed.

Mary came in with a cool, wet washcloth and gently placed it over Lizzie's eyes.

"My dear, sweet Lizzie. Like *mamm* said, this is all going to be all right. *Daed* will come around. You'll see."

Breathing deeply, Lizzie worked at calming herself. Turning onto her side, she hugged her knees to her chest. The cold compress fell away from her eyes. When her sobs finally quieted, she said, "I sold the artwork to help you and *Daed*, *Mamm*."

"Lizzie, when did you start doing this?" her *mamm* asked.

"I started painting soon after David died. After *Daed*'s heart attack, Paul and I came up with this plan to sell my art at his shop. It was the only way I could think of to help bring money into the family. My roadside stand certainly wasn't going to be enough, and there was no man in my life to marry and bring here to live to help on the farm..." She paused for a moment, gathering her thoughts. Her lower lip quivered as she whispered. "Because of the way I look, there will never be a husband for me to bring home to take David's place."

She felt the mattress dip as her sister sat next to her. "Oh, Lizzie! Don't say such a thing! Those thoughts are not the truth."

For a long time Lizzie thought her future as an *alt maedel* was set, and then she'd fallen in love with Paul. Her heart ached. She placed her hand over the spot in her chest where it lay beating. For the briefest of moments she'd felt happiness bursting from inside, and now all hope was once again lost.

"I saw you painting earlier today. I guess I assumed *Mamm* and *Daed* knew you did this."

Lizzie shook her head against the pillow. "*Nee.* I was afraid that they would see my drawings and watercolors as a frivolous pastime. There's always so much work to be done on the farm and I only drew when I had free time. In the beginning I used the drawings to cope with the accident."

Pushing herself up off the bed, she pointed to her dresser. "Go open the bottom drawer, *Mamm.*" While her *mamm* did that, Lizzie bent over, and reaching underneath her bed, she pulled out a box.

She put the box on the bed between her and Mary, flipping the lid open to reveal dozens of drawings and paintings.

"Oh! *Dochder!* Your work is so beautiful!" her *mamm* exclaimed from across the room.

"Look at what you've done," she said, spreading the artwork out in front of her. "I can see why that man wants to buy your work."

"*Mamm*, do you see that box on top of the dresser?"

Mamm nodded.

"Open it up."

Standing, *Mamm* reached for the box. Carefully lifting the lid, she peered inside. "Lizzie! There's over one hundred dollars in here!"

"That is from the sale of my first watercolor. Paul…" Fresh tears sprang to her eyes. Swiping her hand across her face, she took in a determined breath. "He sold one of my pieces last week."

Hanging her head, she added, "I was going to put it with the money from the sale of my jams. I now know thinking I could convince you that I was doing so well with my jams and baked goods was a silly notion. I'm so sorry."

Mamm came across the room to join Lizzie and Mary on the bed. Putting her arms around both of them, she said, "I love both of you so much. And Lizzie, *ja*, you were wrong to keep your paintings from us. You shouldn't have gone against your *vader*'s wishes. We will have to pray to ask for forgiveness."

"Yes, *Mamm*." Even as she agreed to pray, Lizzie found she couldn't get the look on her *vader*'s face out of her head.

She had disappointed and hurt him yet again. Lizzie couldn't bear the thought that she'd brought more pain and, worst of all, shame to her *vader*'s home. The man had been through so much over these past years. From now on she would be a good *dochder*, doing as he asked of her. And if that meant finding a farmer to marry instead of a furniture maker, then so be it.

They all heard the screen door open and snap shut. *Mamm* quietly left the room. That left Lizzie and Mary alone. Poor Mary looked so tired. She didn't need to stay to comfort her.

"Mary, you look exhausted. Go lie down. I'll be fine." Though she used her best confident-sounding tone, Lizzie knew she'd failed in convincing her sister, because they both knew she was anything but fine.

Gripping her hand, Mary said, "You will get through this. We've survived far worse, you know."

"I do know. But this pain—" Lizzie thumped her chest "—that I'm feeling inside here… I've never felt this before."

"It will get better. I promise." Mary pulled her into a quick hug and then pushed her growing figure up from the bed. "I'm going to go put my feet up."

She watched her sister walk slowly from the room, thinking at least one of them had done the right thing. The sound of her parents' voices floated up the staircase. She tiptoed to her bedroom door and opened it a crack to hear what they were saying.

"She went against my wishes. Not only that, she outright deceived us. I'm not ready to forgive Lizzie yet. I need time to think about what she's done."

"Joseph. We both know that Lizzie's heart was in the right place."

"I need time to think and to pray on it."

Closing the door, Lizzie shut out their voices. Leaning her back against the hard wood, she knew what had to be done.

She picked up the paintings, the very ones her *mamm* had been looking at, off the floor, and placed them back in the bottom drawer. Pushing the drawer closed, she straightened up, catching sight of the watercolor of the barn. The one she'd been working on just a few short hours ago. She touched one corner, rubbing her thumb over the image of the lilac bush. It had been in full bloom the day of the accident. The bush had been cut down a few years ago. It had lived out its life.

Her hands began to tremble. Lizzie pressed them together, willing the motion to stop. Her fingers felt so cold. Lizzie shivered. She had more work to do. Ignoring the gnawing inside her stomach, she left the painting on the dresser, turning her attention to the paints and brushes. She kept her mouth firm, quelling the urge to cry again. She picked up the tubes of watercolor paints, bringing them over to the box on the bed. Looking down at the pieces of paper with all those images—some sketched out and some with colors added—she saw her dreams fading away. She let the tubes of paint tumble from her hands to join the tattered drawings. Numbly she crossed back over to the dresser, picked up the brushes and placed them in the box.

She stood there, looking down at the gift of color that Paul had given her. The side of her face underneath the scar started to ache. She brought her hand up, lightly rubbing the area where the skin puckered. She hadn't felt pain in the area in a very long time. Not since the day Paul had brought her these gifts. She had no use for any of this. She folded the cardboard flaps together, then shoved the box as far as her arms could reach, underneath the bed.

If Lizzie had learned one thing from all of this mess, it was that she should have followed her instinct and never left her family's farm. The life she thought she could have with Paul was nothing more than the dream of an innocent heart. Her life, for now, and as it always had been, was right here.

Chapter Fifteen

Paul stood on the Millers' front porch with a bouquet of wildflowers in his hands. The late summer daisies and the lavender he'd found alongside the road fluttered in the breeze. He hadn't seen Lizzie in two very long days. He'd wanted to come earlier but knew she and her family needed time. For him, though, time was running out. Over these past months he'd grown to know Lizzie so well. He knew what made her smile and what made her pull away. It was the pulling away part that had him worried.

She'd given him her heart the other day. And then, just like that, it had been taken away. He stood there on the porch with the bees buzzing in the bushes next to it. A pot clanged in the kitchen. He heard female voices. He leaned in, listening for the sound of her voice. Shuffling his feet, he raised his hand and knocked on the door.

Lizzie's *mamm* answered the door. "Good afternoon, Paul."

"Mrs. Miller, I'm not going to waste any time with pleasantries. I need to see your *dochder*."

"If it's Lizzie you're coming to see, I'm afraid she's refusing to take any visitors at this time."

Expecting this to happen, he said, "I understand. I brought these flowers for her." Extending his hand, he waited for her to receive them.

She took them from him, pausing to smell the fragrant scent. Raising her eyes, she said, "*Danke.* I'll be sure to give these to her."

"Please tell your *dochder* that I still love her." Paul walked away, leaving a bit of his heart behind.

Paul returned two days later, determined to see Lizzie. This time he was met at the door by Mary, who informed him that Lizzie had gone for a walk. He was about to climb up into the buggy when he caught sight of her walking around the far side of the barn. She didn't see him, and Paul used that to his advantage. In a few long strides he stood before her. She came to an abrupt halt in front of him.

Lizzie drew her mouth into a thin line and he thought all might be lost. Then he looked into her eyes and saw her profound sadness. The way he figured it, she wouldn't be looking that way if she didn't still love him.

Not wasting any time, he got right to the point of this visit. "Lizzie, I know you're angry with me. I've come to apologize for what happened the other day. I had no idea that man would come here. I'm sorry he did."

Lizzie sidestepped around him. He spun around, wasting no time in catching up with her brisk pace.

"Come on, Lizzie. Talk to me."

Ignoring him, she kept right on moving, trying to outpace him, which of course was a ridiculous thing to try and do, considering she had to take two steps to his one.

"Lizzie. Please."

Finally she stopped moving. With her back to him, she spoke. "You need to leave."

He shook his head. "I'm not leaving."

"You can't stay where you're not wanted."

"I'm not leaving until you listen to what I came here to say."

He reached out a hand and touched her upper arm, gently turning her to face him. "Lizzie, I love you. And you told me you loved me. I believe, here—" he fisted his free hand, thumping it against his chest, his voice breaking as he continued "—in my heart, that you still do."

Tears rolled down her cheeks. Her mouth tried to get the words out. Finally she managed to say, "I can't love you anymore."

"Lizzie, you can't mean those words," he implored her.

"I should never have let you convince me to continue with my watercolors. By doing so, I've brought nothing but pain and shame into my parents' home." Shaking her head, she said, "I've put my paintings away."

"*Nee*, Lizzie." Over and over he shook his head. "*Nee.* The Lord gave you that talent for a reason."

Raising her hand, she held it out in front of her as if to push his words away. "*Nee.* The Lord would never bring this pain on me. No matter how much I loved you, I can't bear the thought that I broke my parents' hearts yet again. Please don't sell any more of my watercolors. I don't care what you do with them, but don't sell any more."

Then Lizzie ran up the walkway, raced across the porch and hid inside the shelter of the Miller home. Paul could hear her sobs coming from inside the house. Choking back tears, he hung his head. This wasn't how he wanted things between them to end. Without Lizzie in his life, he had nothing. He wasn't about to let her go without putting up a fight. Because he knew *Gott* intended for them to be together. But how could he convince her?

Another three days passed. Three days in which he closed himself off from the world. Standing in the middle of the Burkholder Amish Furniture Store, with his hands on his hips, Paul surveyed his handiwork. Though the spot where the dining room set stood was now empty, his plans were to replace it with a brand-new one. But without Lizzie, the joy he took in working with his hands had dimmed. Without her by his side, he felt as if nothing mattered. He looked at the walls where her watercolors hung.

Fighting back the pain, he walked over to the painting she'd done of the field where they'd had their first picnic. He remembered how excited she'd been seeing the view from the hillside. Paul could still see the way her hand had moved over the page. Brushstroke after brushstroke, she'd created this stunning image with seemingly little effort.

He'd fallen in love with her even more that day.

She'd come so far since then. He'd watched her confidence blossom as she'd been brave enough to trust in her talent and to trust in them. He couldn't let her escape back into seclusion. Lizzie didn't belong on the farm. She belonged out in the world, where she could share her artwork. She belonged with him.

Looking at the yellows and greens, he still felt the awe of her talent.

Her *Gott*-given talent.

He couldn't let her throw this all away. She'd been given that talent for a reason. Just like others in the community created beautiful quilts, Lizzie's hands created lovely watercolors. Her heart and soul were in these watercolors. He knew she'd never be able to forgive herself if she stopped creating art and left all of this behind. Lizzie wasn't meant to be a farmer's wife. She was an artist.

Reaching up, he took the framed watercolor off the wall. He carried it to the back room, wrapped it in brown packing paper, cut a length of string from the spool that hung on the pegboard and then tied a neat string bow on the top. Carrying the painting under his arm, Paul walked out of the shop.

The trip out to the Miller farm didn't take more than twenty minutes, but to Paul it felt as if hours had passed. His insides were telling him he needed to get to Lizzie. When he finally made it to their property, he stopped the buggy next to the barn. His horse pawed at the soft earth. Paul's senses picked up. As he jumped down from the buggy seat, he heard the sounds of crying coming from inside the barn. Quickly he went to the building, peering inside the tall sliding doors. Dust motes danced around his shadow. A woman stood in the middle of the large room. He could see her arms wrapped around her middle. The prayer *kapp* covered her honey-colored hair.

Lizzie.

She gave no indication that she'd seen him. Paul stepped into the dimness, heading straight for her. In long, easy strides he met up with her in the middle of the barn and gathered her in his arms. She nestled her head underneath his chin as he held her close, feeling her shaking. Rubbing his hands along her back, Paul tried to ease her pain.

"Oh, my dear, sweet Lizzie. Please don't cry."

"I've ruined everything," she sobbed into his chest.

"No, no. You haven't ruined anything."

He let her cry some more, holding her as tightly as he could, willing his strength to flow to her. Praying for his own strength. Remembering that horrible day so long ago. The very day that had set their future in motion.

Paul knew that David wouldn't want to see his sister in so much pain. He knew that David would want her to forgive herself.

"Lizzie," he said, taking a chance that he was sharing the things her *bruder* would want her to hear. "It's time for you to forgive yourself. You need to let go of the past…let go of things we can't change."

She continued to cry, shaking her head against his chest.

"Lizzie. You need to forgive yourself. Please forgive me. We've come so far. I can't let you go now. Please don't make me let you go."

"I… I'm so filled with pain. I don't know what to do with any of these feelings."

"Give them up to the Lord. He will protect you and heal you. Lizzie, I know together we can bring the light back."

She stepped away from him. Scrubbing her hand across her face, she looked down at the floorboards. It was then he noticed the crumpled paper. He bent down and picked it up.

"What's this?"

"The picture of the barn I've been working on. The image has been stuck in my mind for so long, I finally put it down on paper. You've seen this…" she said, hiccupping.

Paul worked to smooth out the wrinkled edges, seeing that it was indeed the watercolor of the barn. He focused on the lilac bush.

Tapping the spot with a finger, he said, "This isn't here any longer."

"The bush was there the day David died," she explained. Sweeping her hand out in front of her, she whispered, "I can't do this anymore."

"Wait here—I'll be right back." Taking the picture

of the barn with him, Paul hurried out to the buggy, where he exchanged it for the one he'd brought from the shop.

He came back inside and handed it to her. "Here, open this."

Her fingers trembled as she pulled the string loose, releasing the brown paper.

"Look at this picture." He tapped the glass. "This is the watercolor you painted the day we went on our picnic. I know you remember this day, Lizzie."

She shoved the painting back at him, turning her face away from him. Cupping her face in his hand, Paul had her facing him again. Though he could see her turmoil, he knew he had to convince her that they needed to be together.

"Every painting you do shows your beauty and your strength. The day we went to this field for our picnic, that was the day I fell in love with you. No matter what happens, Lizzie, I will always love you. And nothing you can say or do will ever change how I feel."

"I won't let you love me!" Lizzie shouted as she ran past him, out of the barn.

Clutching the painting in one hand, Paul went after her.

"Paul!" Joseph Miller's voice boomed behind him.

He stopped in his tracks, watching Lizzie moving away from him one more time. He turned to find her *vader* standing in front of the barn doors. He wondered how long the man had been outside.

"*Ja*. I heard what you said to my *dochder*."

"Then you know I love her."

"I do. But I also know you need to give her a little more time."

"I'm not sure I can do that."

The man's bushy eyebrows pulled together as his stare bore down on Paul. He waited.

"I've looked at Lizzie's paintings. I understand why she does them. You are right—she has been given a great talent. I know she's been doing nothing but using it for the good of our family. Perhaps I've been hard on her. These years have not been easy ones, Paul."

"I know, sir."

"I needed her to marry a farmer. Instead she has fallen in love with a furniture maker. One who, I might add, convinced her to keep secrets from her family."

Joseph wagged a finger at him, "Your *vader* and I were very close to going to the bishop over your actions. In the end, though, we've decided your decisions, while misguided, had been made for the right reasons."

Frowning, Paul didn't know if he should apologize or defend his actions and feelings for the man's *dochder*. In the end Joseph was the one to concede.

"Like it or not, my Lizzie loves you. If you can convince her to come back to you, you have my blessing to be married."

Chapter Sixteen

The floor felt cool beneath her bare feet, reminding Lizzie that cold fall air would be settling in before she knew it. Putting on her black stockings and black shoes, she finished getting dressed. Her entire body ached. Not from illness, though. She ached with the familiar pain of loss. Letting Paul go was going to be harder than she'd imagined. Lizzie knew he'd been hurting. They were both hurting. Sighing, she wished loving someone were easier.

From the kitchen she heard the sound of the teakettle's whistle. She went downstairs and found only Mary in the kitchen, padding around with bare feet.

"Mary! You should put on your stockings at least."

"My feet are so swollen. And they feel hot. I'm letting them cool for a bit," Mary explained, turning around to look at Lizzie. "You look tired."

"I'm afraid I haven't been sleeping well."

After walking back to the stove, Mary took two mugs out of the cabinet above it. "Come, join me for some tea. I'll make us up a pot of Earl Grey. I know it's your favorite."

"*Danke*. I'd like that. Are there any muffins left?" she asked, knowing there were some left in the basket when she'd gone to bed last night.

"I think only corn ones. *Daed* took the blueberry ones with him when he left for the fields this morning. Aaron went along to help him with the harvest."

Lizzie accepted the mug her sister handed her. Bringing it under her nose, she inhaled the sweet fragrance of the bergamot oil the tea was known for.

"Come on, let's go sit out on the porch."

"What about your feet? Won't they get cold out here?"

"I'll be fine," Mary replied, laughing.

She joined her sister on the swing. Lizzie looked down at her sister's stomach, noticing the soft rounding of her belly. It gave her a comforting feeling to know that two little lives lay safely in Mary's womb.

"You must be excited about the babies."

Mary's eyes lit up. "We are. Aaron is hoping for boys, but I'd like one of each." She gave her head a slight shake. "*Nee*, that isn't true. I don't care if they are girls or boys as long as they are healthy."

Lizzie rested her head on Mary's shoulder, feeling safe and secure and loved.

"Tell me, *liebschen*, how are you holding up?"

"I'm taking things one day at a time." Lizzie felt guilty at having to admit that.

There was something to be said for life staying on

course. Ever since this change between her and Paul, she could hardly keep up with all of the emotions.

"I understand Paul has come by several times since the incident." Mary pushed her toes against the porch, putting the swing into motion.

"We're calling that day an *incident*?" Lizzie cocked an eyebrow, meeting Mary's gaze.

Mary let out a soft, very unladylike snort. "I don't know what else to call it. Lizzie, do you love Paul?"

Her heart ached so much, she wanted to weep from the pain of it.

In a soft voice she answered her sister, "*Ja.* With all my heart, I love Paul Burkholder."

"Then you need to work this problem out."

"I'm not sure we can."

"Was *Vader* finding out about your artwork really so bad?" Mary wanted to know.

Lizzie shrugged. "On that day, *ja*. It was bad. That man came here, looking for me. The look on his face when he noticed my scar was too much for me to bear. I'm better off here at home. Not out in the world. Besides, Paul is not a farmer."

Mary put her foot flat on the porch floor, stopping the motion of the swing. "You need to stop thinking that way."

"*Vader* needs help on the farm. We can't afford to hire anyone. The money from the art sales would have helped things."

"*Ja.* Maybe so." Mary looked thoughtful for a moment and then she said, "Aaron and I have decided to stay."

"Stay here? For how long?"

"Hopefully for the rest of our lives. We want to raise the twins here, in Miller's Crossing. *Daed* needs the help on the farm, and Aaron is a farmer, after all."

"And Paul is a furniture maker."

"Maybe now you can forgive him, Lizzie. Forgive yourself."

"I'm trying to, Mary. My mind has been a jumble of thoughts and feelings that I've never felt before… I just don't know what to do with it all."

"Lizzie, this is all natural."

"Yes, but is love always this hard? Just when I thought my life was sure to be that of an *alt maedel*, Paul Burkholder, a boy I watched grow into a fine man, comes along and takes my heart."

Mary put her arm around her shoulders, pulling her closely. "Ah, my dear Lizzie. This is a *gut* thing for you. Love is a wonderful part of life. There are so many of us in this community who marry because it's the right thing to do for the family. But we have both been blessed with men who love and cherish us. You need to remember that and thank *Gott* for it."

They sat for a few minutes longer, watching the birds pick at the feeder.

"You need to let your heart open back up and trust what is inside."

"When did you get to be so wise?" Lizzie poked her in the arm.

"I've noticed that being with child has made my senses keener."

Together, they laughed.

"I've missed you, Mary."

"And I you." Resting her forehead against Lizzie's, Mary added, "Now go find Paul and settle this issue between you once and for all so we can get on with planning the next wedding."

Lizzie left her sister on the porch, deciding to walk into the village. She needed the time to think, and the few miles of walking alone would help her clear her mind. As she made her way up the driveway, she noticed that all around her the land seemed to be changing. The fields had turned from green to gold. Here and there on the side of the road were dried leaves. Raising her eyes, Lizzie caught sight of tinges of golds and reds on the leaves, evidence that the seasons were changing.

Spotting a maple tree just beginning to turn red, she imagined how the colors would look on her art paper. She continued walking, trying to put the words Mary had spoken into perspective, realizing how much she had truly missed Paul. The place where her heart was in her chest began to ache. Lizzie rubbed her hand over the spot, wishing she'd never fallen in love. Then she wouldn't know this heartache.

In the next instant she realized how much she missed him. She missed his smile. She missed his touch. She missed seeing the excitement on his face every time he talked about the Burkholder Furniture Store. Even if the Burkholders didn't agree with their *sohn*'s choice, Paul deserved to be a successful businessman. As mad as she was at him, she would not begrudge him that. Lizzie thought he deserved to find happiness, too, just not with her.

She felt a wetness on her face and realized she'd been crying. Swiping a hand across her eyes, she fought back a sob. She couldn't imagine Paul with anyone else, and yet she couldn't imagine him with her. She'd known all along that she wasn't worthy of love. She'd told Paul that many times over. Why hadn't he listened? Why had she given in?

Lizzie stopped moving, spent from feeling sad and lonely and angry. Off in the distance she saw the top of the church spire on Clymer Hill Road. The sunlight poured out of the heavens, making it appear as if it were made out of silver. That place meant so much to her and Paul. Lizzie couldn't explain the feeling washing over her. She had to go find Paul.

The sound of the sander broke through the morning silence. Paul had been out in the shop at their homestead since well before dawn. He'd been busy working off his frustration by finishing a tabletop. The showroom floor looked empty without the dining room that he'd sold to the *Englischer.* Though he'd known when he'd picked this slab out he'd had only one person in mind.

Lizzie.

His plan had been to surprise her with a lovely table as a wedding gift after she agreed to marry him. Now as he stood here amid the sawdust, some of the last words she'd spoken to him rang in his ears.

I won't let you love me, she'd said.

Pressing hard, he slid the sander over the wood, trying to erase their last moments together. The hurt he'd seen in her eyes still brought him pain. The thing was, he couldn't imagine loving anyone else. And now that he'd had time to think about them, he realized he'd always loved her. All those times he'd told himself they were just friends had been nothing more than his denying his true feelings.

"Paul. *Sohn. Sohn!*"

He turned when he felt a tap on his shoulder. *"Daed!"* He pulled the orange foam earplugs out of his ears and shut the sander down.

"I've been calling to you. Guess you couldn't hear me above all the noise."

"Sorry. I've been trying to get this tabletop finished."

Cocking an eyebrow, *Daed* asked, "A special order?"

"*Ja.* What's on your mind?" Paul asked.

"I know things have been strained between us since Rachel and Jacob's wedding."

"Ja." Paul wiped a hand across his brow.

If he'd learned nothing else being Amish, it was the power of forgiveness. He'd been just as guilty as his *daed* in their dealings with the shop, and in the end with the hurt they'd caused each other.

As soon as he'd finished sanding, he planned on heading over to the Miller house. He'd been there three times already, and each time Lizzie had turned away. Maybe today would be different.

After pulling out a stool, *Vader* sat, resting his forearms in front of him on the workbench. "I'm not getting any younger, you know. And life is too short to stay mad at each other."

Paul nodded. "Agreed."

"Do you think we can work our way through this?"

"I do." Reaching out, he captured his *daed*'s hand with his, wondering when it had become hardened with arthritis and roughed with time.

"I understand your need for independence. Maybe I've been a little hard on you these past years. But that's only because I love you. And maybe a little bit because I need you here in the shop. While they're helpful, your *bruders* don't seem to have the passion that you do when it comes to woodworking."

"Ben and Abram don't mind helping out."

"I know. But you have more ambition."

Paul let go of his *vader*'s hand. He blew the sawdust off the tabletop and ran his hand over the smooth cherrywood. "I only want what is best for the family, *Daed*. I would never leave here."

"I know. Perhaps I was afraid you'd be snatched up by some *Englischer*'s company. They pay well from what I hear."

"I'm doing fine with my own furniture."

"I've been hearing talk of your shop. I was at the general store the other day and Mr. Becker told me your shop is getting a lot of foot traffic."

"I've been keeping busy."

"The long and short of it is, I'm fine with you having the furniture shop in the village. And I'm fine if you want to have a courtship with Lizzie Miller. Not that it's my blessing you'll be needing."

Paul grinned. "Joseph already gave me his."

Slapping his hand on the workbench, *Vader* stood, declaring, "Break time's over!"

Paul untied his heavy canvas work apron, took it off and hung it on a hook near the entrance. "I've got to be heading out for a bit."

He had one thing on his mind and that was to find his Lizzie and convince her that they belonged together. No matter what the obstacles, together they could overcome anything. Paul didn't want to waste any more time without her.

Chapter Seventeen

He saw her coming over the rise, her pale blue skirt flapping against her legs. Lizzie was moving at a pretty good clip. Pulling the reins toward him, he rolled the wagon to her, bringing it to a stop along the edge of the road.

"Paul." She ran up to the wagon, out of breath. "I was coming to find you."

"On foot?" He jumped from the wagon and reached for her hand.

"*Ja.* I was going for a walk to think about things... to think about us. And then I saw the Clymer Hill Road church spire. It's so beautiful today."

Looking over her head, he saw the church off in the distance. It surely was one of the prettiest places in the area. "Would you like me to take you up there?"

"If you have time."

He started to say, for her he'd always have time, but Paul was still trying to gauge her mood. Something had changed—that was for sure. When he took her hand to help her up on the wagon bench, she didn't shy away like he expected her to.

Moving to the middle of the seat, Lizzie smiled at him as he settled in next to her.

"It's a lovely day for a ride, don't you think?"

Paul didn't know what to make of any of this. He knew whatever was going on had to be serious. "Lizzie. I'm not sure what's going on here."

"I've something to tell you and I need to say it at our special place."

He led the horse and wagon up the long hill to the church. The wheels rattled over the oil-and-stone roadway. In less than ten minutes they reached the spot. Paul sat in the wagon, staring out at the view, thinking that this was all he'd ever wanted out of his life. His *Gott*, this bountiful earth's beauty and Lizzie.

"Do you want to get down?" she asked.

He saw a shadow of worry in her blue eyes. Putting his hand over hers, he said, "Let's go sit on our bench."

Together, they sat, looking out over the fields and valley, looking toward the horizon. Their fingers were intertwined. They sat that way for a long time, until their breaths came in unison.

Lizzie broke the silence by saying, "I've been very stubborn these past days."

"I hadn't noticed," he teased.

"*Ja.* I think you did. I had a talk with Mary today. She told me some things I hadn't considered before."

"Like?"

"Like the fact that love isn't easy to come by. But when you find it, you should never let it go."

Paul stayed quiet while he thought about how to go about thanking Mary.

Keeping her eyes averted, Lizzie continued. "My life has been a struggle. But a lot of that I put on myself. After David died and I woke up in the hospital knowing my face, my life, would never be the same… I found it easier to keep to myself. To keep all my feelings inside. To let very few people get to know me. The one constant I've had in my life, other than my family, has been you, Paul. And I almost did the unforgivable. I almost let you go. There's one more thing I need to tell you."

Lizzie reached out to take his hand in hers. "Paul. I remember. I remember that last day with David. I don't think any of what happened was our fault. I was going to the barn to get him. I told him we weren't supposed to be there. I remember climbing high up those bales of hay. We were almost touching the rafters. And David, he was talking about flying through the air. I saw him jumping from bale to bale, his little body leaping high between each one. I tried to find a foothold on the next bale. And then we were tumbling. I lost sight of David. Then the next thing I remember was waking up in the hospital."

Paul tried his best to blink back tears.

"I never once thought you were to blame."

"I know, but for years I blamed myself."

Gripping his hands, she gazed up at him. Paul saw her hurt, fear and guilt slip away.

She blinked and then gave him a small smile, saying, "I'm ready to let the past go and look to the future."

He couldn't imagine his life without her in it. But to hear those words coming from his Lizzie…his heart filled with love.

"Lizzie, never once has my love for you wavered."

Paul stood, pulling Lizzie up off the bench. They faced each other as a cool breeze swirled around them. He brought her hands to his mouth and kissed them. Then, releasing them, he cupped her beautiful face in his hands. He ran his thumb along the scar. And then lowering his head, he kissed the roughened skin. She tried to pull away, but he held her in his loving hands.

"I love every part of you. From your head to your toes, Elizabeth Miller. I love you."

"I love you with all my heart and all my soul. With all that I am, Paul Burkholder."

He kissed her, feeling her love and strength. Releasing her, he turned them to face the horizon.

"I think David would be very happy if he could see us together."

He held fast to her hand. "I know he would be."

Gathering her in his arms, he held her tightly. She smelled like sunshine and lemons and love. "Why don't we go give our families the good news about our courtship."

Tipping her head back, she looked up at him, and laughter bubbled out of her. "Are we courting?"

He nodded. "Your *vader* has already given his blessing for our marriage."

Tears sprang to her eyes. "Oh, my. Then I guess our future has already been decided." And they couldn't have been happier.

Epilogue

"Let me see!" Laughter bubbled up out of Lizzie as Paul led her through the door of their new *haus*.

Shortly after Paul had declared his intentions and acquired his *Zeugnis* from the church, with Joseph's blessing, he and Lizzie had gotten married. Lizzie had insisted she only wanted family and close friends at the wedding—not the entire community—which had been fine with Paul. He thought they'd waited long enough.

Paul had finished the dining room table shortly after their wedding. And today he'd be showing his handiwork off to his new wife, who at the moment stood squirming in his arms. Chuckling, he said, "Lizzie, patience is a virtue."

"Hmm." She laughed again. "If I stand perfectly still, can I open my eyes?"

"Yes."

Making sure she was standing in the right spot,

at the head of the table, Paul said, "Okay. Open your eyes."

She let out a gasp, her eyes widening. "Paul! It's *wunderbar*!"

Moving around the table, she took in every inch of his work. The cherrywood top had been a splurge, even though he'd known that pine would be simple and plain, lasting years. Paul had wanted to give his Lizzie something that would last a lifetime. He wanted something that could be passed from generation to generation, long after they were gone to be with *Gott*.

Lizzie began tipping her head this way and that, and then bent to look underneath the table. He couldn't imagine what she could be searching for.

"Lizzie?" he questioned her. "Is something wrong?"

"*Nee.* I'm looking for your mark."

He walked around the table and joined her at the side. Taking her hand in his, he guided her fingers under the table, until they touched the spot where the small circle lay. Rubbing their fingers over the grooves of the brand, he felt the letters *PB*.

They sat down on one of the benches that had been a wedding gift from his family. Other than their bed, the dining set was the only furniture in their two-bedroom home.

"I have a gift for you, too." Lizzie stood and then disappeared into the bedroom. She returned with a flat package.

"Open it."

Paul tipped his head, giving her a curious look. He

tore the tape off the wrapping, lifted the paper away and then gasped when he saw the watercolor.

"I know you loved that barn painting, and I destroyed it. Lucky for both of us, I remembered all the details."

Running his fingers along the edges of the barnwood frame, he felt at a loss for words.

"Ben did the frame for me," Lizzie admitted. "I thought we could hang this above the mantel in the living room."

"I think that would be a fine place. I'm sorry the room is so empty."

"Paul, I'm not worried about the furniture," Lizzie assured him as she returned to her place next to him on the bench.

"If I'd had more time before our wedding, I could have made you some more furniture."

Lizzie pulled him toward her and kissed him soundly on the mouth.

Lifting her head, she said, "It wouldn't matter to me if our *haus* were empty, because as long as we are together, these walls will be filled with love."

* * * * *

If you loved this story, check out these other books set in Amish country

The Amish Widower's Twins *by Jo Ann Brown*
His Suitable Amish Wife *by Rebecca Kertz*
A Perfect Amish Match *by Vannetta Chapman*
Her New Amish Family *by Carrie Lighte*

Available now from Love Inspired!

Find more great reads at www.LoveInspired.com

Dear Reader,

A Love For Lizzie is my debut novel with Love Inspired. As my characters Lizzie and Paul went on a journey, so did I. This was my first time writing an Amish story. I discovered that the Amish community is built on traditions, faith and family. And even though their life is lived simply, the Amish have their share of life's trials and tribulations. Paul and Lizzie have to overcome many obstacles, including trusting in their faith in God and in each other. Though my book is set in a fictional town called Miller's Crossing, the actual area is based in beautiful Chautauqua County, also known as the Southern Tier of New York State. As you read this book, imagine rolling hills, dotted with barns and acres of open farmland.

You can learn more about me by visiting my website at www.traceyjlyons.com, or stop by my author page www.Facebook.com/TraceyJLyonsAuthor. I love hearing from my readers. You can contact me at tracey@traceylyons.com.

I hope that you enjoy reading Lizzie and Paul's story as much as I enjoyed writing it.

Welcome to Miller's Crossing!

Happy Reading,
Tracey

Double Treat Cookies

This recipe makes 8 dozen cookies.

Ingredients

2 cups all-purpose flour
2 teaspoons baking soda
¼ teaspoon salt
1 cup butter (2 sticks) softened
1 cup of granulated sugar,
plus ¼ to ½ cup reserved for shaping
1 cup packed light brown sugar
2 large eggs
1 teaspoon vanilla extract
1 cup creamy peanut butter (or for extra crunch
you can use 1 cup chunky peanut butter)
1 cup chopped salted peanuts
1 6 ounce package semisweet chocolate chips

Preheat your oven to 350 degrees F.

1. In a medium bowl, sift together the flour, baking soda and salt.

2. In a large mixing bowl, beat together the butter, sugars, eggs and vanilla until fluffy. Then blend in the peanut butter.

3. Add the dry ingredients to the butter and sugar mixture.

4. Stir in the chocolate chips and the peanuts.
5. Shape dough into small balls about 1½ inch in diameter, then place them 3 inches apart on ungreased baking sheets.
6. Using a glass, dip the bottom in the reserved granulated sugar and flatten each cookie.
7. Bake until brown, about 8 minutes. Transfer cookies to wire rack for cooling.

These cookies can be stored in a container and will stay fresh for up to five days. You can also use butterscotch chips in place of the semisweet.

COMING NEXT MONTH FROM
Love Inspired®

Available July 16, 2019

THE AMISH BACHELOR'S CHOICE

by Jocelyn McClay

When her late father's business is sold, Ruth Fisher plans on leaving her Amish community to continue her education. But as she helps transition the business into Malachi Schrock's hands, will her growing connection with the handsome new owner convince her to stay?

THE NANNY'S SECRET BABY

Redemption Ranch • by Lee Tobin McClain

In need of a nanny for his adopted little boy, Jack DeMoise temporarily hires his deceased wife's sister. But Jack doesn't know Arianna Shrader isn't just his son's aunt—she's his biological mother. Can she find a way to reveal her secret...and become a permanent part of this little family?

ROCKY MOUNTAIN MEMORIES

Rocky Mountain Haven • by Lois Richer

After an earthquake kills her husband and leaves her with amnesia, Gemma Andrews returns to her foster family's retreat to recuperate. But with her life shaken, she didn't plan on bonding with the retreat's handyman, Jake Elliott...or with her late husband's secret orphaned stepdaughter.

A RANCHER TO REMEMBER

Montana Twins • by Patricia Johns

If Olivia Martin can convince her old friend Sawyer West to reconcile with his former In-laws and allow them into his twins' lives, they will pay for her mother's hospital bills. There's just one problem: an accident wiped everything—including Olivia—from Sawyer's memory. Can she help him remember?

THE COWBOY'S TWIN SURPRISE

Triple Creek Cowboys • by Stephanie Dees

After a whirlwind Vegas romance, barrel racer Lacey Jenkins ends up secretly married and pregnant—with twins. Now can her rodeo cowboy husband, Devin Cole, ever win her heart for real?

A SOLDIER'S PRAYER

Maple Springs • by Jenna Mindel

When she's diagnosed with cancer, Monica Zelinsky heads to her uncle's cabin for a weekend alone to process—and discovers her brother's friend Cash Miller already there with his two young nephews. Stranded together by a storm, will Monica and Cash finally allow their childhood crushes to grow into something more?

LOOK FOR THESE AND OTHER LOVE INSPIRED BOOKS WHEREVER BOOKS ARE SOLD, INCLUDING MOST BOOKSTORES, SUPERMARKETS, DISCOUNT STORES AND DRUGSTORES.

LICNM0719

SPECIAL EXCERPT FROM

What happens when the nanny harbors a secret that could change everything?

Read on for a sneak preview of The Nanny's Secret Baby, *the next book in Lee Tobin McClain's Redemption Ranch miniseries.*

Any day she could see Sammy was a good day. But she was pretty sure Jack was about to turn down her nanny offer. And then she'd have to tell Penny she couldn't take the apartment, and leave.

The thought of being away from her son after spending precious time with him made her chest ache, and she blinked away unexpected tears as she approached Jack and Sammy.

Sammy didn't look up at her. He was holding up one finger near his own face, moving it back and forth.

Jack caught his hand. "Say hi, Sammy! Here's Aunt Arianna."

Sammy tugged his hand away and continued to move his finger in front of his face.

"Sammy, come on."

Sammy turned slightly away from his father and refocused on his fingers.

"It's okay," Arianna said, because she could see the beginnings of a meltdown. "He doesn't need to greet me. What's up?"

"Look," he said, "I've been thinking about what you said." He rubbed a hand over the back of his neck, clearly uncomfortable.

Sammy's hand moved faster, and he started humming a wordless tune. It was almost as if he could sense the tension between Arianna and Jack.

"It's okay, Jack," she said. "I get it. My being your nanny was a foolish idea." Foolish, but oh so appealing. She ached to pick

LIEXP0719

Sammy up and hold him, to know that she could spend more time with him, help him learn, get him support for his special needs.

But it wasn't her right.

"Actually," he said, "that's what I wanted to talk about. It does seem sort of foolish, but…I think I'd like to offer you the job."

She stared at him, her eyes filling. "Oh, Jack," she said, her voice coming out in a whisper. Had he really just said she could have the job?

Behind her, the rumble and snap of tables being folded and chairs being stacked, the cheerful conversation of parishioners and community people, faded to an indistinguishable murmur.

She was going to be able to be with her son. Every day. She reached out and stroked Sammy's soft hair, and even though he ignored her touch, her heart nearly melted with the joy of being close to him.

Jack's brow wrinkled. "On a trial basis," he said. "Just for the rest of the summer, say."

Of course. She pulled her hand away from Sammy and drew in a deep breath. She needed to calm down and take things one step at a time. Yes, leaving him at the end of the summer would break her heart ten times more. But even a few weeks with her son was more time than she deserved.

With God all things are possible. The pastor had said it, and she'd just witnessed its truth. She was being given a job, the care of her son and a place to live.

It was a blessing, a huge one. But it came at a cost: she was going to need to conceal the truth from Jack on a daily basis. And given the way her heart was jumping around in her chest, she wondered if she was going to be able to survive this much of God's blessing.